Z-d

A guide to surviving the Zombie apocalypse in Great Britain.

Written by Mark Long, Illustrated by Shane Feazell.

© Mark Long and Shane Feazell, 2013. All rights reserved

First Imprint, eBook and hardcopy, 2013

Cover composition and some artwork produced by Arc Media Associates (http://www.arcma.co.uk/).

The print copy of this book has been sized to fit in your "Go" bag.

Index

Important!

If there is a zombie apocalypse happening right now, this is the section for you. If you have time to prepare, go to section 2 for advice on how to do this.

1. WHAT TO DO RIGHT NOW.

You don't need to be told that this is a bad situation. My job is to help you to deal with it. The first things that you need are not weapons or food. The first thing that you need is time to make good choices. A bad choice can kill you. The enemy is not a strategic planner. Your choices will determine whether you live or die.

So, find somewhere that will be safe for at least a short time. Do not find a defensible place and barricade yourself in because you can be trapped there. For now, the ability to run matters a great deal. Zombies used to be people so where there were few people, there will be few zombies, at least in the initial stages. You need to find somewhere fairly deserted which is easier than it might seem in a crowded country like the UK. At all times, consider the risk of being trapped. If you are trapped, you have few options. If you can flee, you can regroup and reassess. The next few days or weeks are going to be a constant stream of decisions if you are to survive.

Unless you are in a safe place, you will need to travel. Use whatever means are available at this time but avoid crowded and enclosed places as much as possible – the London Underground, even if it is still running, will be very high risk. If there is still a large human population, be aware that others will be trying to do the same. You may need to choose your destination based on where you can get to. This is discussed in more detail later.

If you are in the city:

Offices are likely to be fairly deserted, especially if the outbreak happened at night or society is already in chaos. People are unlikely to be going to work during a major outbreak. If the outbreak happened at night or during a weekend or holiday, offices are especially likely to be empty. There may be some useful supplies there and there is likely to be more than one exit. Fire safety regulations insist on this. Consider all possible exits and entrances. Windows that open or that can be smashed can be a way for them to get in or for you to get out although modern office blocks have shatter-proof windows that cannot open. There is significant cover in an average office – places to hide or complex cubicle layouts that will slow down a mentally impaired attacker. Offices are not a bad choice.

Shops can contain useful supplies even if it is not immediately obvious what they have to offer. They also have multiple exits and generally have reasonable physical security to prevent criminals from entering and stealing stock. They are unlikely to have many people in them so the number of zombies should be low. However, they are a very attractive target for looters. If you are not alone and have enough companions to keep control of a shop then this may be a good choice. You may be able to persuade looters to join you. However, this is a higher risk option. A shop may better as a base of operations after you know what you are going to do and when there are fewer looters.

Homes are generally a poor choice because there are or have been people there. If the people have become zombies, there are now zombies there. The natural tendency of people when threatened or ill (infected) is to go home. I do not recommend this choice although you will probably want to forage for supplies there later.

Vehicles could be a good choice as they are the one hiding place that you can move but there is a problem. In cities, traffic can be a problem at the best of times. If there is still a significant human population, they will be fleeing and the roads will be blocked. If the human population is largely dead (or undead) then there will be abandoned vehicles blocking the roads. It is all too easy to be trapped in a vehicle and getting trapped is likely to get you killed. Vehicles are useful in many situations but they can be a liability in a city. If petrol is available, there may be completion for it or active fighting. If the power is out, the pumps will not be operational.

Factories may contain useful supplies and equipment that could be of use. Like offices, they have multiple exits. They may contain food or industrial equipment that can be used for protection or as weapons. However, this may be too heavy for easy transport or even immobile. An otherwise useful item that slows you down can kill you if you need to run.

Police stations may seem potentially useful. They have reasonable physical security and may have weapons. If society is still partially functional, the police are likely to try to protect you. While they have not been trained in how to handle zombies, they are likely to be well intentioned and capable of functioning under pressure, at least when compared to other survivors. However, there is an important consideration here. If you go to the police for help (assuming that there are police) then you will have lost control of your options. They will be in charge and you will be required to trust your life to strangers. There is a high probability that the police will be overrun if they are trying to exert some measure of control. They will be involved in human-zombie interactions and the risk of infection is high. Accordingly, a manned police station is likely to be a poor choice. An abandoned police station could be more useful, especially if you are the first person there. They are likely to have things that you need such as guns and riot gear. However, the cells are not a good option. While they are wonderfully secure, they have no way out that is not the way in. If the station is attacked by zombies or looters then you have no way out. Avoid the cells!

Restaurants might seem like a good option but probably are not. There is food there which is good. However, much of it will be fresh food that will spoil quickly especially when power and refrigeration is lost. They tend to be in places where there are people; their business depends on it. The smell of food may attract zombies. Restaurants are better considered as places to raid than places to set up a base or to seek refuge.

Hospitals may appear to be an attractive option due to the ample medical supplies but this is a very poor choice. Hospitals are crowded places. They are where the sick and the injured are taken. Dead bodies are stored at hospitals. During an outbreak, they will be flooded with wounded who will soon rise as zombies. Avoid these places at all cost.

If you are in the countryside:

There are fewer people outside of the towns which is a major advantage. While there are fewer buildings, they tend to be working buildings – they have a purpose. Food comes from the countryside. Roads are more likely to be passable. In many ways, this is a much better survival option. You will probably have a little more time to think.

Farms generally have several types of building and the nature of these buildings will vary according to the type of farm. All farms will have equipment sheds and storage sheds. Arable farms (that grow crops) will have more storage sheds than farms devoted to livestock. There will typically be at least one house with possibly some smaller cottages. If the farm is abandoned, these can be good places to hide and take stock of the situation. If you are with a group then it is possible that you can hold a farmstead as a longer term base. However, there are some possible problems that you should be aware of. The first is that modern farms are not designed to be defensible and fire safety regulations do not apply to them in the same way. There may not be multiple exits from places. It is possible to be trapped. Many buildings are designed to be secure enough to prevent livestock entering or leaving but may not be safe against zombies or other survivors. The livestock may attract zombies. Animals make noise and smells. Unhappy animals make even more noise and even more smells and if untended or frightened, they will be very unhappy indeed. Animals can represent a threat even if they are immune to the zombie plague – which is not something that you will know in the early stages of an outbreak. If the noise or smell attracts zombies, you could be sitting in a target. Accordingly, while this is potentially a good longer term solution, it is a probably a poor choice for an initial place where you can consider your options.

Homes tend to be more widely scattered in the countryside but the same caveats apply as for the city. Home is where people go when they are ill or scared. Where there are homes, there are typically people. In an outbreak, unprepared people are likely to become zombies and therefore a threat.

Factories in the countryside tend to be either small workshops (potentially useful) or large industrial plants within commuting distance of a large town. The latter is potentially a problem as zombies can get from the population centre to the factory. However, it is likely that zombies will prefer to keep near their supply of food (which is to say people) and this will keep them largely in population centres until the food (people) runs out. Accordingly, factories or workshops in the countryside are not bad places to hole up while you consider your options and may be useful as longer term bases of operations.

Vehicles are essential to life outside of the city because homes, workplaces and shops are further apart and less public transport is available even when there is not an emergency. The nature of the vehicles is often different. Off road vehicles powered by diesel are both common and useful. Roads are unlikely to be blocked. While the fuel lasts, the archetypical "Chelsea tractor" 4-wheel drive vehicle is likely to provide a mobile base that you can use for a reasonable degree of personal safety. They are fairly resilient to attack from zombies, can move away from larger groups, can travel around blockages in roads, offer shelter against the elements and can carry a useful amount of supplies. In the countryside, this is an excellent choice and does not have to be abandoned if you find a more permanent base. Fuel will become an issue but that is dealt with in a later chapter.

Natural terrain, while not a building of any kind, can offer a degree of protection. The nature of this terrain will depend on where you are in the country. Woodlands are common to most areas. These offer concealment (you can't see the survivor for the trees), firewood, raw materials (wood) and are likely to contain game and may, depending on the season, offer nuts, berries and mushrooms. In medieval times, outlaws and peasants lived in woodland for years. This can accordingly be a very good choice. Downs and moorland offer very little in the way of cover or resources. About the best that can be said of these is that they are deserted and you can see anything that is coming your way. Fields, while not natural terrain, offer only one advantage over downs and moorland and that is that they may have crops although these may not be edible or in season. Beaches are not typically useful. If they have a cliff then there is a risk that you will be trapped on a narrow strip of land with the sea to one side (effectively impassable for most people) and a cliff on the other. These should be avoided although coastal regions will have boats that can be helpful. This is discussed in the transport section. While the concealment offered by natural terrain can be of help, it may also prevent you from seeing zombies entering the area. However, they are less likely to enter an area if they cannot detect anyone to eat in there.

What do you need once you are out of immediate danger?

Your needs are, in order of urgency:

1. Safety

2. Water
3. Heat
4. Food
5. Everything else

We have become used to a world where food and drink are as close as the nearest McDonalds. That world has gone away. Whether it comes back depends on who survives.

While these are discussed in more detail in the section on supplies, here is a very brief guide to help you until you get to that section:

Bottled water is widely available as are soft drinks. It is likely that water supplies will continue for some time after an outbreak because the process is largely automatic. However, as time goes on, the risk of contamination will grow. The water in the pipes at the start of an outbreak is probably safe so you should be able to fill any available bottles with water. Any sealed bottles of water are safe but water from other sources such as streams and lakes may be contaminated. Boiling water for at least 10 minutes will kill many bacteria and most viruses. It will not kill prions. Since we do not know what the disease agent that causes zombism is, we cannot be sure that it will be effective against this disease. Since prions often affect the brain, it seems likely that the disease agent will be of this type. However, boiling water will still protect against a range of other infectious agents.

Heat is necessary for survival but how urgent this need is very much depends on the season. An exposed person can start to suffer from hypothermia within minutes under the worst conditions that are found in Britain. Being wet or in contact with wet ground will speed up the process considerably. People who are exhausted are more likely to suffer from hypothermia in cold weather. However, you can generate heat by moving at the cost of calories. You can keep heat in with suitable clothing and even wet clothing is better than no clothing at all unless there is a considerable breeze in which case a dry layer like an emergency blanket can be a life saver. It is best to have too much clothing. You can take off something that you do not need but not put on something that you do not have.

Food is essential in the longer term but you can go for several days without eating if you have to. The body stores energy in the form of fat and a compound called Glycogen which is in the muscles of the body. Once that runs out, you will have problems but it is enough to keep you alive for a reasonable time while you look at options. You should not take unnecessary risks to obtain food unless you are literally starving. Hungry is not starving but you may feel faint after missing a meal or two. This will generally pass as your body starts to metabolise stored carbohydrates and fat. You will be vulnerable until this period of weakness passes.

As for everything else, that can and should wait until you have got the basics of water, heat and food.

Once you have found a place where you will be safe for at least a few hours and you have water and heat and food, it is time to start thinking about strategy. What you have been doing up to this point is tactical. You have been dealing with the situation as it is. Strategy is about the longer term. For advice on that, see the following chapters. If you do not have time to read each section (and I recommend that you do when you can) then use the index to get to the section that you need.

2. Preparation

I hope that you are reading this in a safe warm place and that there is plenty of time to prepare. If you are reading it by candlelight while checking out of the window for zombies then your objectives are the same but it will be a lot harder to achieve them.

The most important piece of preparation that you can do is not a material thing but a mental thing. You must think, and you must think in specific ways that promote survival. On a minute by minute basis, you need to evaluate the risks inherent in each action. Before Z-day, a trip to the local shop to buy sugar was a safe thing to do. When zombies roam the world, each action must be considered in terms of risk versus reward. Is it worth exposing yourself to that level of danger for that goal? That is a tactical decision. Strategic decisions are longer term and must relate to minimising the number of times that you are exposed to risk for the things that you need.

It is said that the first casualty of war is the truth. Well, that may be so but most soldiers would say that the first casualty of war is the plan. Things don't go the way that you would expect and you will probably have to adapt the plan to suit the circumstances but you cannot adapt something that you do not have. Plan for the worst case scenario and assume that you can modify your plans if you are lucky enough to find that things are better than you expect. So, what is the worst case scenario? I will discuss this in chapter 3, called "WHAT CAN YOU EXPECT", but the one thing that you can be sure that you will have is yourself. You must make yourself as useful as possible if you are going to survive.

Many survival guides recommend building up large stocks of supplies. American guides in particular recommend preparing a large weapons cache. In Britain, most weapons are simply unavailable and I believe that it is unlikely that you will be able to stay in your home. Having 200 gallons of petrol stockpiled is of very little use if you have to flee on foot because the roads are clogged with abandoned cars. I do recommend having a "go" bag packed but the majority of preparations that you can make are based on skills and knowledge. The plan is part of that knowledge. A fall back plan is a sensible precaution.

So, the plan should include, as a minimum, the following:

1. Where are you going to go? Remember that there will almost certainly be other survivors. If the location that you are planning on going to is not one that can be readily shared or if the other survivors are not willing to share it, you will need a secondary location. There are certain types of location that panicking survivors will certainly go to and unless you want to fight them, you would be well advised to make other plans in case they do not wish to cooperate. Supermarkets and gun shops will be stripped pretty quickly. In the section on equipment, I will suggest other places to obtain what you need.
2. How are you going to get there? The section on transport will be a useful guide.
3. What will you take with you? The "Go" bag is a given. What else will you take if you are on foot? What if you have a vehicle? What will you abandon if you have to lighten the load? These are all things that you can decide ahead of time.
4. Who are you going to take with you, assuming that they

survive? If they don't, is there someone else that you should take? Do you want to involve other potential survivors in planning for Z-day?
5. What skills do you need?

With regard to skills, they travel with you. Some of them need special equipment but the equipment may be small and portable or you may be reasonably confident that you can acquire it at a later date. In the case of some skills, you may be able to make it from available materials. Here are some skills that you may want to consider.

First aid. This is a useful skill under normal circumstances. In an outbreak, hospitals are going to be one of the first places where things will get out of control. In this situation, this skill becomes vital. Fortunately, this is a something that you can get for free. Organisations such as Saint John Ambulance or Red Cross will train you. You will be expected to stand a few duties and treat some casualties but try to think of it as advanced practical training. Alternatively, many employers are willing to train staff in being first aiders to meet regulatory requirements. Simple injuries can become crippling if not treated and this skill will help you and make you valuable to any survivors that you meet. If you are valuable to the group, your survival chances are increased.

Lock picking. At first glance, this doesn't seem like an obviously useful skill when force can be used to break in any door that you need to open. However, one problem with this is that anyone or anything can then get into the building. If you are raiding for supplies, you run a serious risk of only being able to use a particular location once. At best, you run a risk of zombies being there next time that you need it. If you are looking for somewhere to rest or a more permanent base, it is essential that you are able to secure the building once you are inside. Picking the lock is by far the best way of doing this. It also has the advantage of not making it obvious that there is anyone inside the building. There are a variety of types of lock picks ranging from the simple and light 20 piece pick set (a small leather wallet of tools) to the bulkier and noisier pick guns. You will need to learn how to use them but there are a number of useful books explaining the techniques including the free MIT Guide to picking locks by Theodore T Tool. However, practice is the best teacher. It is legal to own lock picks in the UK but illegal to carry them without good reason such as being a locksmith. After Z-day, it is unlikely that the legality of carrying them will be a problem.

One or more low technology skills. In the modern world, many basic techniques are all but lost. Butter comes from the supermarket. Leather comes as shoes or jackets. Learning how to make things from available materials is a skill that will stand you in good stead if there is no rescue or recovery in sight. Colleges often have courses in leather working, pottery and similar subjects. Some traditional organisations have basic blacksmithing classes and there is a wide range of information online. The ability to create things from available materials will make your life more comfortable if you survive and will again enhance your value to a group.

Archery. While bows may not be very effective weapons against zombies (see the section on weaponry), they can be used for hunting. Arrows can be reused and can be made. Modern arrows have carbon fibre or aluminium shafts which are difficult to manufacture. If wooden arrows are used, only the heads require specialist smithing techniques. The shafts can be turned with a simple bodger's lathe. If you don't know what a bodger's lathe is, that is all the more reason to learn a low technology skill. You may not be able to find a ready-made bow but a self- bow can be made from readily available materials.

The essence of the skill set that you develop is to enable you to survive in a world where society no longer supports you. Short term survival may be enough to get you through if the outbreak is limited and help will come. If the outbreak is prolonged or so widespread that no help comes, you will need the skills to survive and pass on.

What to pack in your "go" bag.

This is what I have in mine. You may want to alter the contents of your based on your skills or needs.

- Bandages. They go out of date so I replace them when they are within 6 months of expiry.

- Rubber kitchen gloves. These offer minimal protection but are light. Surgical gloves are lighter and pack small but they are less robust. They are excellent for infection control, a topic discussed later in this book.

- 2 bottles of water. Good for cleaning wounds, washing off possible infection and drinking.

- 2 packs of Kendal mint cake. It keeps for ages and has a very high energy density.

- 2 emergency (space) blankets. These are remarkably effective and light. If you are wet, a single blanket can stick to you and so not help to insulate you. However, using a second one will form an air gap making it very much more effective.

- A bottle of sanitising gel.

- A hunting knife of the type sometimes called a Bowie knife. This is not for fighting zombies but simply because a knife is very useful. It can be used to skin game, make kindling or a hundred other things.

- Small roll of duct tape. This is just generally useful.

- Chemical light stick.

- 2 cigarette lighters. These tolerate getting wet better than matches and the ability to make a fire can make a lot of difference in comfort and your ability to survive in winter.

- A roll of lockpicks.

- Soap.

- A small scale map.

- A windup radio with headphones. Batteries can go flat and a device that causes noise at your position is a potential liability.

- This book.

None of this equipment cost more than £50. Most of the items were under £5. The bag is a small rucksack that weighs less that 5 KG (12 lb in old money). It is nowhere near everything that you will need in the long term but it is a lot better than having nothing. You can base your kit on mine or choose what you want but I would advise against packing anything too heavy. Since you ideally want to have it with you whenever possible, I would also advise against putting anything illegal in there. The Bowie knife and lockpicks are problematic and the police typically take a dim view of anyone who carries surgical gloves. While none of this matters after Z-day, you really don't want to be in a police cell when things go bad.

If you have a family, you will want to prepare a "go" bag for each of them. While it is a good idea to have a wider range of equipment, the basics should be the same for each bag so that if one is lost, there are still supplies of that item left. If you have room, you should consider taking high energy long lasting foods such as rice or pasta. Metal drinking mugs are light, unbreakable and can be used for basic cooking. Solid fuel stoves (Hexamine is a common brand) are small, light and cheap. It is well worth considering one if you have the room. They are available in camping shops and military surplus stores.

So, skills and a "go" bag are the minimum that you should expect to have during an outbreak. Could more be done to prepare? It certainly can, but let us consider the dream scenario. You have a place already prepared in the countryside, well away from population centres. It is stockpiled with canned goods with long expiration dates, seeds, weapons and other gear. You have 5 friends who know of its location and each of them has useful skills and between you, you cover a sufficiently wide spectrum that you believe that you could keep this base going as a viable community in miniature. It is either already fortified or can be fortified in short order. I think that you will agree that this is an ideal set-up. It is what disaster recovery specialists would call a warm site which means that you could go there and be operational within a day or two. However, we have to consider how practical this is. There are problems:

1. There simply are not many sites like that. England and to a lesser extent Scotland, Wales and Northern Ireland are densely populated areas. There is very little land that is cultivatable which is not already in use. There is woodland that could be cleared but this is neither easy nor quick. If as few as 100 groups tried to set up such locations, the supply would be exhausted.
2. Setting up a site like this would be expensive. Realistically, you would need at least 5 acres of defensible land. At the time of writing, properties like that sell for around £500,000. Spread between your team of 5, that would be £100,000 each. In practice, who has that sort of money spare? There would also be considerable upkeep cost.
3. The assumption here is all 5 of your team would survive. While their chances are greatly increased because they are prepared, it is unlikely that all of them would make it because of simple bad luck. If you assume the worst case, only 1 or 2 of the team will survive the first 24 hours. You would struggle to maintain a base of that sort with so few people.
4. Other survivors are likely to try to take over your prepared position. This can be prevented by fortifying the property ahead of time but that is neither cheap nor easy.

It may be that you have the resources to maintain such a site for however long before it is needed but if so, you are very much in the minority. If you can do it then your chances of survival are very much better. Hopefully, the advice in this book will still be helpful to you. For the vast majority of us, we simply don't have that level of resources and we will have to react and take advantage of whatever happens to survive.

It may be that you already live in a place that could be defended. There are three factors to consider. The first is how high the zombie threat is likely to be in the area where you live. Most of us live in population centres. It is likely that, after Z-day, there will be a high population of zombies in densely populated areas in the time shortly after a rapid spread of the infection. The second question is how defensible the house itself is. Upper floor flats are relatively easy to defend but there is no feasible escape route and there is certainly going to be a high population density. Being trapped in a flat is a recipe for slow starvation unless the water fails first. The third consideration is the availability of supplies. It is certainly possible to stockpile a significant amount of food and water but that gives a definite time limit on the suitability of the location. If you have enough ground to grow crops, you are in a position to have renewable food supplies although you will of course need staples to keep you alive while the crops grow. However, unless the boundaries of that land are secure, you will be facing a threat from zombies and survivors whenever you plant, harvest or weed. This is a risk that you want to avoid as much as you can. Accordingly, it is fairly unlikely that your current home will prove suitable.

If you can obtain and transport more equipment than your "Go" bag then you will have an advantage. I will be covering useful equipment in a later chapter. Some equipment may be obtained by salvaging from sites and from people less well prepared or armed. I do not recommend attacking other survivors (see "Interacting with other survivors") but we cannot afford to let usable equipment go to waste. The dead have no need for any gear.

One question that I have not addressed yet is how long the

emergency will last; should you plan for the short term or the long term? The answer is that it depends on the nature of the event. If it is a true apocalypse then help may be a long time coming or it may never come. If it is a localised outbreak then help may come in days or weeks. However, this is not something that you can know ahead of time and you need to plan for the worst case. If rescue comes, they will find you well fed and healthy. If rescue doesn't come, you will still be well fed and healthy. It may be that you will one day be able to rescue others.

What to expect during an outbreak is covered in the next chapter.

3. What To Expect In The Case Of An Outbreak

While it is normally difficult (at best) to predict the future, there are some aspects of an outbreak where we can be reasonably confident that we can know what to expect. It is likely that an outbreak will move through a series of phases with each one having different opportunities and threats to deal with. Here are some possible scenarios and the effect that they will have on society. Throughout this, I will be assuming that the initial outbreak or outbreaks are within a city. There are two reasons for this. The first is that it is the most likely scenario since most people live in larger towns and cities within the UK. The second is that it is the worst case scenario. An outbreak in a city is both the most dangerous and the most difficult to handle. An outbreak in the countryside might be handled by a farmer with a shotgun if patient zero were identified in time. We should always prepare for the worst case.

Stage 1: Isolated outbreaks. You may have heard of recent cases in the US where people were attacked and killed by individuals that were apparently mindless and who ate the flesh of their victims. The US police shot the attackers who continued to feast even when threatened by armed police. The attacks were in Florida and Maryland. These turned out to be humans who (at least in one case) were hallucinating after taking a drug with the street name of "Cloud 9" aka "Bath salts". However, the initial stages of an outbreak are likely to look very much like this.

An outbreak at this level is containable with proper infection control and a rapid response. However, the UK is not the US. The police are rarely able to respond with armed force that rapidly. If they are able to respond and shoot the zombie, infectious body fluids are likely to become aerosolised, spreading the infection. If the zombie is wounded or subdued by force of numbers, they are likely to be taken to hospital. Any victims certainly will be, including the dead. The potential for the spread of the infection is massive if the incident is not handled properly. It is unlikely that the outbreak will be recognised for what it is.

If there is an isolated outbreak and you are not directly involved (which will be true of the majority of the population) then there is no threat unless the infection escalates. It is at this point where you need to go from being aware of the possibility of a threat to being ready to react to an escalation of that threat. You need to check your "Go" bag and if you have a prepared location, you may want to go there and check that the stocks are in a good state. If you can, it may be a good idea to plan to spend a few nights there.

If there are multiple apparently isolated outbreaks then it is likely that they are related and the infection is spreading through a vector that is not yet publicly understood. If the incidents are geographically dispersed then it is probable that the outbreak is more widespread with cases just beginning to come out of the incubation period. In this case, you should seriously consider gathering additional resources in a vehicle if you have one and avoiding highly populated areas. It will be much easier to act at this stage before there is general alarm. This would also suggest that the incubation period of the as discussed in more detail in the section on ... prevention and control.

At this stage, the general population may be a little nervous but there is unlikely to be widespread panic. If all goes well, the outbreak may be prevented from spreading. However, it is likely that it will spread to the victims of the attacks at least and it may be that the attacker was not patient zero – and this becomes a certainty if there are multiple attacks. Additionally, there may have been other attacks that went unnoticed since a missing person may not reported, especially if they were vulnerable and little regarded such as those that sleep rough on the streets of towns and cities. The victims of these may become zombies and spread the infection further. You should monitor the news very carefully and bear in mind that any official statements are likely to be intended to reassure the population. There may be tell-tale signs such as increased arming of the police or even mobilisation of some army units. These may not be reported in mainstream news so blog posts, twitter and social networking sites may give the first information to indicate that the situation is escalating.

Stage 2: Multiple attacks and the beginning of a coordinated response. At this stage, it is certain that there will be official advice offered by the government. They will advise people to avoid unnecessary travel, to stay in their homes and to let the police and (if mobilised) the army do their work. Hospitals will be calling in additional staff. Organisations such as the Red Cross and Saint John Ambulance will be called to assist. If you have joined one of these organisations, you are likely to be notified via this channel. If you believe that the outbreak can be controlled then you should consider helping. If you believe that the outbreak is already too advanced to be contained, you will want to turn your efforts toward personal survival.

There will be considerable alarm in the general population. They are likely to ignore official advice, the British public being what it is, and will head away from effected areas. If you have tried using the British roads on a bank holiday weekend, you will know that there is very little spare capacity. It is likely that the roads will become increasingly impassable so if your plan involves leaving the area where you live, doing so as early as possible is a good idea.

One factor which is likely to complicate matters is that information is likely to be incomplete or incorrect in parts. People may not know whether the areas that they are fleeing to are any safer than the areas that they are leaving. Outside of the population centres, there will not be housing for the number of people leaving the city. Some will sleep in their cars but it is likely that village halls and other public spaces will be made available. Unfortunately, this means that there are people moving from areas that have known infections to crowded places with inadequate sanitation. It is reasonable to assume that infection will be spread further in this way.

As the situation escalates, the official response will increasingly be military in nature with the armed forces patrolling the streets or, as the situation deteriorates, responding to reports of zombies. As the outbreak spreads, reservists will be called up. Recent history has shown that the British military are stretched thinly at the best of times with many troops stationed abroad. Even with reservists, their numbers will probably be insufficient to control the outbreak and they will be just as prone to infection as anyone else. It is also likely that there will be communications issues since the army and police have different communications systems and reservists may not be familiar with current systems. Other groups that are pressed into service as the threat escalates will be less well trained and even less familiar with the protocols. The official response will become less organised and less effective as the outbreak spreads. Attempts to restrain and treat the infected will be replaced by orders to shoot them. Bodies will probably be burned.

One factor which may spread infection is people hiding the infected. Once it is known that the police or army are shooting those who are showing symptoms or who have become zombies, people will not want to report a family member as a victim since that will certainly result in their destruction. Sadly, it is certain that no cure will be known at this stage. It is possible that a cure will never be known. What these people have not learned and what we must remember is that a relative who has been infected is not that person any more. They are not a person at all once the disease takes hold. Cases like this will probably result in the entire family being killed or transformed into zombies. Typically, this will happen in homes, in residential areas. This will result in further deaths as the victims become the danger.

It is still possible that the outbreak is containable at this stage if the disease agent spreads more slowly and the incubation period is short. If infection is via close proximity only and good infection control protocols are followed and the outbreak is limited to a relatively small geographic area then a well-planned response may be able to contain the incident although the death count is likely to be high with casualties among those trying to limit the infection (military and medical staff mainly) being critical. As these staff are lost, so are the skills in tactical control and infection control. I believe, in practice, that it is almost certain that our defences will be over-run. Given that you are prepared, you should certainly not be in any area where this is happening. The best thing that you can do is work on your own survival and plan to assist other survivors when you can.

Stage 3: Resistance is overwhelmed. The level of zombie activity reaches a level where there can be no coordinated response from the authorities and the army and police are no longer trying to control the larger situation. The military will probably, if possible, retreat to a defensible position where they will be besieged. If they carry infection with them, this will be ill advised.

It is important to consider how the zombie "life cycle" (if I may use that term) alters the economics of a conflict. In a conventional war with humans on both sides, the forces become weaker over time as casualties rise and fatigue and loss of morale takes its toll. In a zombie-human conflict, this is still true of the human side. However, because humans become zombies, the zombie forces grow stronger with time as long as the infection rate is higher than the attrition rate. They do not become fatigued. They do not have morale, only a terrible hunger. Conversely, the armed forces are being asked to fight a group increasing composed of their deceased and mutilated comrades. While there are many weaknesses to the zombie as an enemy (discussed in the next chapter called "Know your enemy") in the initial stages, they have significant advantages over an unprepared humanity.

By this time, the remaining population of affected cities will be trying to leave the cities by any means possible. There will be a number of infected among those fleeing. The zombies will, by now, be properly described as a horde. As the number of survivors within the city drops and the zombie numbers grow, the zombies will also start to spread out from the city. The result of this is all too predictable.

The roads will clog with the sheer number of people and cars. Vehicles will break down, many of them overloaded as people try to take as many of their possessions as possible when they flee. There will be collisions. There will probably be some infected becoming zombies within the fleeing crowds. There will, in short, be chaos. For most people, they will not be going anywhere quickly. Most will stay with their vehicles. Some will be sleeping in them.

The expanding ring of zombies will reach the trapped humanity and carnage will result. The deaths weaken the humans and strengthen the zombies. Survivors flee in panic. Many will be killed in the stampede. Many will carry infection further from the city.

If you have heeded the advice in the preparation section, you will not be in this group. If you have found this book in abandoned vehicles and can hear screaming and it is getting closer, get off the road, head away from the mass of people and go and read chapter one as soon as it is safe to do so.

Stage 4: Apocalypse.

The end will not come all at once. There will be civil servants holed up in a cold war bunker somewhere. There will be army camps that will survive for a time. Power stations will continue to run for a while and while they do, there will still be a mobile phone service. There will even be some internet access for a few days. Systems will fail slowly as long as the power remains. Automated systems will go wrong with no-one to tend them. The engineers who make a complex society possible are probably not all dead. They may even be over-represented in the survivors given their interests. However, they will be doing the same as everyone else; just trying to survive.

Over the course of the next few days or weeks, humanity will become a minority. Zombies will roam this green and pleasant land. Political parties will no longer matter. No-one will care who won on X-factor. Your job will almost certainly not exist anymore.

You have a new job and it is the same for you as it is for any survivor. You must survive. While your individual survival is important, our survival as a species is more important still. You will almost certainly have to work with others and that presents challenges that may be new to you. I will offer the best advice that I can to help you with this. A fundamental part of your job is to know the enemy. You must learn to predict how zombies will behave. You must learn which strategies work best for you. You must learn to survive in this new world.

You might think that living in this new world means that you will have some hard choices to make. In fact, there is only one choice to be made: Whether to survive or not. All other choices are just part of that choice. Should you risk entering a town to forage for food? It is part of the same decision. Should you take a stranger into your group? Part of that same decision.

However, it is not just your survival. It is the survival of the human species. It is not a responsibility that you asked for but it is one that you have.

One question that we cannot answer ahead of time is how long the outbreak will last. The emergency is self-limiting to a degree. Depending on the type of zombie and whether they will hunt food other than humans, the number of zombies will probably be much reduced within six months to a year. That is survivable with care and a little luck. Will help be coming? It may be that the outbreak is localised to the UK and help will come from Europe or the US or even Russia or China. It may be that they are affected more severely than the UK and help will not come for years if it comes at all. When help comes, it is unlikely to be friendly soldiers coming to rescue survivors. A military solution imposed from the outside is going to be concerned with removing the threat with as little danger to the armed forces of that nation as possible. If they come, they will be using weapons just as dangerous to you as to the zombies or more so. Fuel bombs are cheap and devastating. Cluster bombs would be an effective way of clearing large areas although it is likely to massively spread infection. If help comes, it is critical that you make it as obvious as possible that you are not zombies and you will have to hope that they care.

What if help does not come? Let us imagine a Britain where 95%+ of the population is dead. The survivors will be people who have done whatever they needed to do to survive. They will probably have little trust in any form of government after the failure of society. It is all too likely that the country will become a collection of feudal groups or an effective anarchy. It will be a world very different from the Britain that we have come to know. Even after the last of the zombies, it may be just as dangerous. Accordingly, we must plan for the long term. We must assume that we have no-one to rely on except ourselves. This may be overly pessimistic. There may be rescue from another country that will try to help civilians. It may be that people will band together and a cooperative new society will form. If so, none of the planning that you have done will be wasted and it will have kept you alive to see the end of the zombie threat. You will be contributing to a new Britain. If the worst comes to the worst... well, we always plan for the worst case. You will survive.

4. Know Your Enemy.

The Chinese military writer Sun Tzu wrote "It is said that if you know your enemies and know yourself, you will not be imperilled in a hundred battles; if you do not know your enemies but do know yourself, you will win one and lose one; if you do not know your enemies nor yourself, you will be imperilled in every single battle." While these words were written over 2500 years ago, they are as useful and relevant as they ever were. Of course, they are far from complete. He also said "He who knows when he can fight and when he cannot will be victorious". To know when we can fight, we must know the enemy.

The term "zombie" comes from the Mbundu word "nzumbe" meaning a corpse animated by magic. One thing that we can be certain of is that the zombies that we will face are not animated by Voodoo but some other factor, almost certainly a disease. There are precedents. The parasitic wasp *Zatypota sp. nr. Solanoi* is a native of Costa Rica. It injects a larvae into a particular species of spider and this larvae literally takes over the brain of the arachnid. The spider weaves a special type of web for the wasp and then dies providing food. There is a type of Baculovirus that infects certain caterpillars and causes them to climb trees where they die and shower infection down on the ground. A major factor in the recent and marked drop in the number of bees in the US is larval stage of a parasite called *Apocephalus borealis* that enters the body of a bee through a wound and causes an infected bee to head towards a light source and wait there. We know that such diseases are possible. It should not surprise us when we find that there is one that preys on humans.

One lesson that we can draw from the precedents is that the disease is always highly specific to the host. Only one species of spiders is controlled by the parasitic wasp for example. This is because the attack relies on controlling the genes of the victim. Accordingly, the disease agent that causes humans to become zombies is unlikely to affect other species although some of the great apes, especially the Chimpanzee, may be prone to infection. However, there are few non-human primates in the UK and that need not concern us.

So, what can we expect zombies to be like? Physically, they will be the same shape as people. This is a problem because it may be difficult to tell the difference between a human, a corpse and a zombie from initial appearance alone. Behaviour will tell us more than a quick visual examination can. In another way, it is helpful. An opening too small for a human will be too small for a zombie. Mentally, we can expect them to be vastly inferior to a living human. Even simple locks are almost certain to be beyond them. Depending on their type, they may be virtually mindless.

Popular fiction suggests two types of zombie. I have decided to call these the Sprinter and the Shambler.

Sprinter: These are not truly undead in that they still have life processes although these may be significantly altered from what we would consider normal. They are zombies only in the broadest sense of the word. Sprinters are likely to be less intelligent than an unaltered human but much more so than the classic shambling zombie. They are much faster, less affected by cold and less affected by wounds. We can draw parallels between the Sprinter and humans affected by PCP aka Angel Dust or more formally, Phencyclidine. This is a street drug that was popular prior to the 1990s in the US. It was never especially common in the UK. This drug, in certain dosages and for certain people, causes a loss of pain response, extreme paranoia and psychotic rage. There are stories of users punching through the windscreen of a car or mutilating themselves under the influence of the drug. One famous case involves a rapper known as Big Lurch who cut open and partially devoured his roommate. We can expect Sprinters to be resilient to pain and fatigue with a moderately increased strength. An uninfected human will not normally exert enough force to damage him or herself; we feel pain and stop. A Sprinter will not have this same limitation. Sprinters are also likely to be able, in the short term, to withstand damage that would disable an uninfected human. The most useful precedent here is the berserker warriors of the Vikings. This quote from the scholar and historian Howard D. Fabing is most descriptive:

"This fury, which was called berserkergang, occurred not only in the heat of battle, but also during laborious work. Men who were thus seized performed things which otherwise seemed impossible for human power. This condition is said to have begun with shivering, chattering of the teeth, and chill in the body, and then the face swelled and changed its colour. With this was connected a great hot-headedness, which at last gave over into a great rage, under which they howled as wild animals, bit the edge of their shields, and cut down everything they met without discriminating between friend or foe. When this condition ceased, a great dulling of the mind and feebleness followed, which could last for one or several days".

From the description, could this have been an earlier outbreak of a temporary form of Sprinter zombism? It is likely that we will never know. One thing that is common to all the reports is that the berserks would fight on with injuries that would have stopped a normal man. If we draw parallels with the Sprinter, wounds to limbs are likely to only slow the Sprinter down unless the trauma is massive enough to cause hydrostatic shock (discussed under the section on projectile weapons). Wounds to organs in the abdomen are likely to have little effect, at least in the short term. Destruction of the brain will prove immediately fatal. A wounded deer can run several hundred metres after a shot to the heart but the injury will be fatal in a short time. Massive blood loss (for example, from a severed limb) will be rapidly fatal with unconsciousness following the loss of blood pressure. It seems very likely that the biological processes that power a Sprinter are similar to or essentially the same as those that occur in an uninfected human.

Shambler: This is the classic zombie that we have come to know from fiction. It is not truly alive or truly dead. We can fairly use the term undead for the Shambler. Physically, they initially appear to be a normal human although obvious wounds will be common. They will decay over time although the rate is likely to be much slower than in an uninfected corpse. Decay will often start at open wounds and internally from the intestines moving outward. Shamblers in an advanced state of decomposition will often be bloated with the gasses of decay. Their level of ability will decrease as decay progresses. Mentally, the Shambler is almost mindless and it will not be capable of advanced reasoning; the brain is a complex organ that deteriorates rapidly. This is the main advantage that you have over the Shambler. Simple tricks will often work repeatedly such as a noise maker at a distance to distract them or traps set in the same place multiple times. Shamblers also move more slowly than humans meaning that they can be outrun. However, the other advantages belong to the Shambler. They do not get tired. They do not need to sleep. They are immune to pain and most forms of damage. If they can inflict a wound that would normally be non-fatal, infection will kill the victim. Because the Shambler does not have a working circulatory system, blood loss or damage to most organs will have little or no effect on them. They do not have any pain response and, as discussed in the section on weapons, pain is a major factor in the ability of weapons to disable a human. Weapons that inflict hydrostatic shock will have less effect on Shamblers because they contain less fluid.

The only sure method of destruction is to destroy the brain. They are likely to be able to continue after a certain level of brain damage caused by (for example) a blunt weapon. They are likely to be, at least initially, stronger than humans because they will use amounts of strength that will harm them. As decay progresses, their strength will diminish. In short, they are hard to kill and they keep on coming night or day and even a scratch from them is likely to be fatal. After the apocalypse, they are also legion. We can only guess at what biological processes power the Shambler. They are apparently anaerobic since there is no blood supply to carry oxygen. They are likely to work at lower temperatures than human metabolism because the processes that heat a living body are largely based on oxidisation of carbohydrates. It is likely that they will function more slowly due to this lower temperature and slower still if it is a cold day.

So, which type of zombie should you expect? I am a firm believer in planning for the worst case and, as some other authors have, I will assume that newly infected humans become Sprinters and when they die from injuries or from the disease become Shamblers. I will also assume that reasonably fresh corpses can become Shamblers. Where the different types of zombie require different treatment, this is specifically called out in the text. Should you only face Sprinters or Shamblers then the advice relevant to that type is all that will apply.

5. *Fighting Against Zombies – How To Do It And Why You Shouldn't*

Many guides to surviving the zombie apocalypse are American. These guides tend to take a rather gung-ho approach to the subject and assume that you have a large stockpile of guns and ammunition. While I understand that guns and ammunition are in much greater supply in the US than they are here in the UK, I still think that this is a poor approach.

Imagine if you will that you have a pistol. In order to have a concrete example, let us assume that it is a Glock 17 semi-automatic pistol. The largest standard magazine holds 13 rounds. The calibre is 9mm which gives the pistol a respectable amount of stopping power with the right rounds (see the section on ammunition). If you listen to American rap, you will probably have heard this pistol spoken of with some respect and it is an exceptionally good hand weapon adopted widely by European forces. Let us consider how an encounter would probably go. For the sake of argument, let us assume that you are in a sub-urban area and that you are as skilled as an American policeman. Please consider that last point. As a civilian, it is very unlikely that you have the same level of ability with a pistol as a trained professional.

This is the Glock 17C. The Slide stop lever is used to allow the slide to be moved manually and should not be confused with the Slide lock which is used to remove the slide while stripping the gun. The trigger safety is a trigger within the trigger and must be pressed to enable discharge of the weapon. It is designed to prevent accidental discharges from objects catching the side. The Glock 17 became standard issue for the British Police's armed response units and the British military in early 2013.

The following figures are from actual encounters, specifically from the Virginian Police department:

"In 1992 the overall police hit potential was 17%. Where distances could be determined, the hit percentages at distances under 15 yards were:

Less than 3 yards	28%
3 yards to 7 yards	11%
7 yards to 15 yards	4.2%

So, if you are as accurate as a professional that has been trained and has spent time practising at a range and in simulated combat conditions, you can expect 2 or, if you are very lucky, 3 rounds of that 13 round magazine to hit your target.

If you are facing a Sprinter, 3 hits would have a fairly good chance of dropping the zombie since you are most likely to hit the torso. Destroying or significantly damaging the heart of a Sprinter will probably kill it, at least until it rises as a Shambler. If your target was a Shambler, hits to the torso will have little effect but they move more slowly and so you may be more accurate. Let us say that you were again lucky and that you managed to get a head hit and this has have taken down your Shambler. You are now standing in a suburban area with an empty gun and you have fired 13 very noisy shots.

They can probably be heard over a range of at least 800 yards. It is very likely that any zombies in that area will be attracted by the sound, especially Sprinters. If you have a spare clip then you will be in the same position in 13 rounds time except that you will have fired 26 shots and anything that didn't hear you the first time will certainly have heard you now. If you have to reload the clip that you have, it will take a minimum 60 seconds during which time you are vulnerable. That is only 4.1 seconds per round. If your hands are cold or shaking (and remember that you have just been in a fight for your life) then it could take easily twice that time. You could well be facing 3 or 4 zombies by this time. You will probably not win.

There is also the question of ammunition. A 9mm round weighs around 8 grams. The ammunition required to destroy 1 zombie using the figures above weighs 136 grams not counting packaging or the ammunition clip. Enough ammunition to kill 10 zombies weighs 1.3 KG. Even if you had access to unlimited ammunition, you simply cannot carry that much of it. Soldiers typically carry around 210 rounds although these are the lighter 7.62mm or 5.56mm rounds. Given that it would be difficult to find ammunition, it is unlikely that you would have that much.

The figures above are quite discouraging. Could they be unduly pessimistic? I have assumed that you are as skilled as a professional and that you have a remarkably good pistol and that you are facing a single opponent at optimal range for a pistol. These are clearly ideal conditions. However, zombies do not fire back and so you could take more time over shots if you can remain calm and Shamblers move more slowly than most humans. Let us be wildly optimistic and assume that you can manage twice that accuracy. That will give you 4 to 6 hits per clip. You could manage to take out (with luck) 2 zombies per clip. In a zombie apocalypse, there will be at potentially dozens of zombies for every survivor. There could be hundreds. A direct confrontation may go your way several times but you have to be lucky every time. They only have to be lucky once.

Unfortunately, it is almost inevitable that you will have to face zombies in combat. The advice in this chapter is based on maximizing your chance of surviving such encounters and minimizing the number of times that you need to do so.

Since it is clear that firearms are not going to help very much even in the unlikely event they are continually available, we need to consider what weapon is more effective and the answer may surprise you. The Russians believed that their greatest asset in war was "General Winter". Enemies in the field would freeze to death. Your greatest weapon is time. If you can survive then time and nature will do what a heavy machine gun cannot.

Sprinters have a life process of a sort. They require fuel to keep moving. They get this from food and much of their food will be human. It is possible that they will also eat animals or other food that they encounter. However, they do not create more food. Sooner or later, they will run out. They may turn on each other or they may not but they will eventually starve to death regardless. They may rise as Shamblers after this happens. Shamblers will not starve but they do decay. Birds and insects will attack them although both decay and animal predation will be less of a factor in winter. They will become less effective with time and will eventually fall apart. If you can survive until this happens then you will have won. There will be new infections from former survivors who managed to hold out for some time after the initial wave of attacks but these will be relatively few. If they come back as a Sprinter (i.e. they are alive when infected) then they will find limited food supplies. Over time, the zombie population will drop and, under the right conditions, it could drop rapidly. Sprinters are likely to be reasonably sensitive to cold and may suffer from hypothermia. While Shamblers do not feel the cold, freezing will damage tissues even as it slows decay. A frozen zombie is not an effective one. A thawed zombie is a damaged one.

So, we need tactics that will help us survive encounters with zombies in the short term and a strategy for minimizing the number of times that we need to survive encounters in the longer term. In a fair fight, you are at a disadvantage because you are much more fragile than a zombie. They can infect you and you cannot infect them. You are going to be very much more sensitive to pain and shock. You are going to be afraid while they are incapable of fear. In a fair fight, you will lose. Accordingly, we must do everything possible to ensure that any conflicts are as unfair as possible.

Before entering into any combat with a zombie or any situation where you are at risk of a combat with a zombie, there are questions that you need to answer. The first question is "Does the reward justify the risk?" The second question is "Could I get the same reward from somewhere else at a lower level of risk?" It may be helpful to consider some concrete examples.

Scenario 1: You have found a supermarket that has not been extensively looted. There are literally tons of foods in there. You are hungry. You know that there is at least one Shambler in there. You have an axe, a combat knife and a pistol with 3 rounds remaining.

Clearly, the potential for reward appears to be very high. There is enough food to last you for months in that shop. However, how much of the food can you realistically take? If you have a vehicle and if you had time then you could fill the vehicle with canned and dried foods. Is it likely that you would have time to do so before more zombies showed up? Could there be more than one zombie in the store? The reward here is actually much less than it seems because you will only get a small proportion of the food. It could be well worth the risk if you had a large vehicle and a force sufficient to hold the building for several hours while you load the vehicle. The risk-reward equation is much more favourable for a group but for a person working on their own, especially one on foot, the risk is higher than the reward justifies.

The second question is still relevant. Is there another way to get the same level of reward for less risk? In this case, there certainly is. What is needed is as much food as you can reasonably carry. Many houses will contain at least this much food, although they may contain zombies and in a well-populated region they may be more dangerous than a large shop. While a supermarket is a big and fairly open space, a house is a series of relatively small rooms with doors. It should be possible to find a house with no zombies in them since we can reasonably expect them to leave an area that has nothing that they would regard as food. This is an option but possibly not a better one. Alternatively, food gets (or more accurately at this point, got) to supermarkets in lorries from warehouses. Warehouses or distribution centres are typically outside of highly populated areas for economic reasons. There will be lorries stuck on motorways with tons of food inside. It may be possible to obtain all of this food simply by driving the lorry away. There are better options here than a one man raid that will certain involve combat with a Shambler.

Would the decision still be the same if you were better armed? The risk would be reduced but the second question is the critical one here. If there is a lower risk option, that is the one that you should take.

Let us consider another scenario. You are in a built up area and it is towards the beginning of the outbreak. You come across a sandbag emplacement. Of course, the point of such an emplacement is to provide cover against incoming fire which zombies do not offer but old habits die hard. There are the bodies of several soldiers around the emplacement complete with rifles. There is one Shambler feeding on a corpse. You are not armed.

What is the risk here? The zombie is clearly the risk. The reward is apparently multiple rifles. Clearly being armed is very much better than not being armed when there are zombies roaming the streets.

Is it likely that you will be able to find the resource that you need elsewhere at a lower risk? In this case, probably not since rifles are likely to be in short supply.

If you can get rid of the Shambler, retrieving at least one weapon is probably fairly simple. However, facing a Shambler while unarmed is clearly very high risk. You could wait for it to move on although there is a level of risk in staying in one place. You are certainly going to want to divide your attention between the Shambler and any new threats entering the area. You could perhaps create a diversion by causing some noise elsewhere that would attract the Shambler. I will discuss some ways of doing this in the equipment section. For the sake of the exercise, we will assume that the Shambler leaves to seek fresh prey, either real or diversionary. What are the risks now? That is the question that you need to ask yourself when facing a new situation or when a situation changes. This has to become more than a habit. It has to become the way that you think. Possible risks that still remain include:

It is unlikely that a single Shambler would have killed multiple armed soldiers. They were probably overrun by many zombies. The others may still be close.

One or more of the soldiers may rise as a newly turned Shambler.

The weapons may have no ammunition. This is more likely that might initially seem the case since you would expect a group of soldiers to be able to resist a reasonably robust zombie threat if they still had working weapons.

If the Shambler leaves, it is probably a good decision to try to get at least one rifle. If the soldiers appear to be dead, you can loot them for ammunition although there is an infection risk inherent in this. So, the initial risk was unacceptably high and then became lower when the Shambler left. There were still some remaining risks but these were risks that could be managed if you remained alert. There probably was not a lower risk option available.

You will face many of these situations in practice and you will need to evaluate the risk versus the benefit for each one. If you are a survivor, you will have to do so hundreds of times. Inevitably, you will make some poor decisions but with luck you will come out of them alive and wiser. One final piece of advice in this section: If you miss an opportunity, it probably will not kill you. If you take an unnecessary risk then it may well kill you. You get multiple opportunities but only one life. It is definitely best to be cautious.

Risk Reduction Tactics.

Wherever possible, you should minimise the risks that you are facing. The keys to this will be observation and planning. You cannot plan effectively without knowledge and you cannot know unless you observe. When entering a situation, you should have a plan for getting out of it. This requires considerable discipline but it also offers your best chance for survival. Some examples may help.

You are entering a building. Things that you should know include how many zombies are in the general area, whether there is evidence of other humans in the area, whether there are any zombies observable in the building (with sight, hearing and smell all being senses of observation), what obstacles are likely to impede your movement within the building, what entrance you will be using and what other exits there are to the building. When you know these things, you have choices. You can plan to enter and exit via the same route but be aware that you have another option if the situation changes rapidly. You could plan to enter the building from one side and leave from the other but that means that you would be entering an open area that may have changed since you last looked. You can plan to back out of the building if things are not as you expected inside because of additional threats. You can even consider whether you can secure parts of the building as you go if you know that the thing that you need is in a particular area.

Of course, this takes time and that may be a luxury that you don't have if you are fleeing from danger. When you do have it, I recommend making the most of it. When you have to make decisions in a hurry, the lowest risk option will often prove to be the best one.

One of the best things that you can do to reduce risk is to improve your ability to observe and the best way to do this is work with another survivor. Soldiers on patrol typically work in pairs or multiple pairs. Two people can look out for each other. Each can help the other if the situation looks bad. One can cause a diversion by making noise and leading zombies away from his buddy. If there is combat, two people stand a much better chance against a single opponent and are less likely to be overrun if there are multiple opponents. If you are lucky enough to have projectile weapons, one can reload while the other shoots. Teaming up with a buddy opens up a range of new possibilities.

Of course, it takes practice to work with a partner. The temptation is to duplicate effort and both watch in the same direction or to target the same zombie. Communication is the key to any successful partnership. Two people working as a team are not twice as effective as a single person; the gain is much more than that. A four person team is much more effective again.

Much has been written on the subject of small squad tactics; the first works to address the subject come from China and date back to the 6th Century BCE. However, much of the advice applies only to symmetrical combat where both sides are armed with similar weapons and both sides have broadly the same capabilities. Here, the battle is not for territory or resources but for survival. The sides are strongly asymmetrical. It would be insanity for the humans to use the same tactics as the zombies. The threat posed by the humans to the zombies and vice-versa are fundamentally different. As a result, the guides on squad deployment and covering fire and so on will not apply well to conflicts with Sprinters and Shamblers. They could apply to conflict with other survivors but, as discussed in a later chapter, you have more in common with even the most hostile survivors than you do with the zombies. The tactics that you develop for use against the zombies will have to be based on what works in that environment for that team. These are some basic suggestions for small teams with the smallest team being the buddy pair:

1. You do not have eyes in the back of your head. Your buddy can see if anything is approaching from behind. If he or she is doing this, they should be in the safer position. You should look back to check that the area where they are not watching is clear as well. Your buddy can tell you when it is safe to do so.

2. Communications are the key but shouting is bad. Even short range radios are better than nothing. This is discussed in the section on equipment.

3. Vital resources should be shared where possible. For example, if you have medical supplies and one of the team has experience that makes them better able to use it then they should carry some of the medical supplies. They should not carry all of them because they may be lost or they may be injured and need assistance themselves. Survival is not just about survival of individuals but also the survival of the team.

4. Teams enable you to have watch rotations. Sleep is essential if you are going to be effective.

5. Vehicles make more sense when you have a team. For rapidly getting out of a situation, having a driver in the vehicle and ready is a great help.

Cover is important in conventional combat partially because it shields you from incoming fire. When facing zombies, there is no incoming fire and their only option is to close to hand-to-hand range where they have a distinct advantage. However, cover is still important because it helps you to remain undetected. You cannot become invisible unless you are wholly behind cover but you can avoid being obvious. Any time that you are against a lighter background, you are obvious – this most commonly happens when you walk along a ridge or a raised structure in the city and is referred to as skylining. You are obvious when you make a noise. You are less obvious when you are in shadow. You are less obvious when you do not move. Cover should be used for concealment rather than material protection. I suggest that you observe the activities of nearby zombies carefully so that you will be aware when they notice you and what the trigger was. While it seems unlikely, they could be aware of body heat or the smell of a living human. The better you understand your enemy, the better you will be able to avoid or defeat it.

Similarly, anywhere that a zombie could be hidden will need to be checked. Shamblers are certainly not going to be intelligent enough to use cover intentionally but they can be lucky enough to be out of sight from the angle at which you are approaching. A shambler with lower body injures may drag itself along the ground making it difficult to spot. Sprinters may be able to understand the basics of using cover. You should assume that any area that you cannot see into may have a zombie in it. This is easy to say but difficult to do. However, it is possible to get better with practice and you can start well before Z-day. As you are walking around, plan out how you would approach the area in front of you to check for zombies that are not in plain sight. Consider where they could be laying or standing. Work out if you could back out of a confrontation if there was one behind that van or behind that garden wall. The sooner that you start thinking like this, the more natural it will seem and the better you will be able to apply the skills when there may actually be zombies there. As a side effect, it will make it very difficult for anyone to mug you.

Is there a good reason to hunt zombies? Well, yes, but only under some very special conditions. In general, the best strategy is to avoid the enemy. Where the risk of facing the enemy is outweighed by the benefit, you should minimise the risk and the combat as much as possible. Why would you seek out combat with zombies? In practice, survivors are unlikely to have much effect on the population of zombie in a large area when the better trained and equipped police and army have failed to do so. However, when setting up a safe enclave, it will be necessary to clear the area of zombies. Some suggested techniques for doing this can be found in the section on setting up a permanent base.

6. Vehicles And Getting Around Post Z-day

Unless you have the luxury of starting in a location that is safe and sustainable in a zombie apocalypse, you are going to have to travel. Even if you do have a location like that, it is likely that you will need to leave to forage for supplies or to look for or pick up other survivors. There are going to be some new challenges to moving around in a post-zombie world and these will vary according to where you are and how you are travelling. I will address the differences for each method of transport.

I am assuming that towns and cities will have few survivors and a number of abandoned or crashed vehicles blocking roads. There will probably have been an attempt by the majority of the population to leave cities and that this would be partially successful at best causing people to proceed on foot. Cars will have crashed when injured and possibly infected drivers lost control of vehicles. There may even be wrecks of vehicles where the army fired on them to try to prevent looting or to prevent possibly infected people leaving an area. It is also likely that there will have been fires in some areas causing roads to be blocked by rubble. In the smaller towns, it is likely that more of the population would have been able to leave and so the roads there will be less congested with fewer vehicles blocking the road. However, this will depend on the speed of the spread of the infection. If the spread is slower, towns are likely to be relatively empty and zombies will roam the countryside killing the people who have fled the towns. If the spread is more rapid, the towns will be jammed with vehicles, some of which contain trapped zombies.

It is of course illegal to take a vehicle without the consent of its owner. It will remain so after the zombie apocalypse but it is very unlikely that there will be police officers in the area after Z-day and any that are present are likely to have other priorities at that point.

On foot

Inevitably, some of your travels will be on foot. There are places where you cannot reasonably get a vehicle such as the inside of buildings. The disadvantages are clear: you will move relatively slowly, you will have no protection against any attack and you will be limited in what you can carry. The advantages are equally obvious. You don't need any equipment for this, you don't run out of fuel and you can get pretty much anywhere this way if you can spend the time.

When travelling on foot, you need to be especially aware of your surroundings since threats can be found anywhere and you may not be able to outrun them. Shamblers are slow but they don't need rest. Sprinters are fast, possibly faster than you if you are not in great physical shape or if you are carrying a heavy load. Observation will help you to avoid situations where you have to run even if it means that you will miss some opportunities to gather resources or search an area for survivors. Basic tactical doctrines will help here.

In built up areas where roads are blocked with abandoned

vehicles, this is one of the few options that can be used. In the countryside, you have more options and walking is less practical because things are further apart. A 10 minute drive can be a 4 hour walk.

If you have to run away and you are carrying heavy things that you can live without, drop them. You may be able to come back and get them later. They may distract the zombies or survivors chasing you. The things that you drop will be of no use to you if you are dead.

Bicycle

This might not immediately seem like a good option but it has many of the advantages of walking and nullifies or at least reduces many of the drawbacks. If you have a bicycles, you can still travel in towns where roads are blocked since the bike can move between cars or on pavements (sidewalks for American readers) and even within some buildings such as shopping centres. Fuel is not an issue because the bicycle is powered by you. With panniers, it is possible to carry a respectable amount of cargo with a relatively small loss of speed. A bicycle enables you to move faster than Shamblers and possibly Sprinters although it does take a few seconds to mount the bicycle if you are on foot and get up to speed. The bicycle is also very quiet allowing you to move through infested areas without necessarily alerting the zombies in the area.

An average speed of around 15 MPH is possible with an ordinary bicycle and a very moderate level of fitness. This may not seem impressive if you are used to driving cars but that would allow you to travel 60 miles in 4 hours compared to 16 miles on foot. The speed record for a human powered bicycle is just less than 83 MPH. A good racing bike should give you speeds of over 30 MPH for short periods which is faster than an athlete can run. If you can avoid meeting a zombie head on, a bicycle should allow you to move through infected areas in relative safety. You can cover 40-60 miles a day in reasonable conditions without pushing yourself especially hard since that is only 3-4 hours riding. However, bicycles offer no real protection against weather or attack if something catches up with you. You will need additional food since you are the power source for the bike. The cargo capacity is limited and normal bikes can only take one person. Tandems are rare, more difficult to use and less flexible.

Fortunately, bicycles are easy to come by and are very unlikely to have been the target of looters. Homes, specialist bike shops, larger supermarkets and car part suppliers are all likely to have at least a few bicycles and some will have a good selection including accessories such as lights and panniers. Before you dismiss the bicycle as an option, it is worth noting that the Swedish military have bicycle infantry units.

There are a few basic types of pedal powered bike:

BMX: These bikes are designed for tricks and stunts and typically have a very basic gearing system making them unsuitable for longer rides and higher speeds. Many of the cheaper models are very poorly built.

Mountain bikes: These are all terrain bikes and have suspension and wider tyres with treads designed to work will on muddy surfaces. They are slower and heavier than some types of bike but are not a bad choice for a post-apocalypse Britain, especially outside of towns or where the roads have deteriorated.

City: This is the classic bike with fairly straight handlebars and a sturdy frame and these can be found almost anywhere – the "Sit up and beg" design as they have been called. They are well suited to riding on paved surfaces and are reasonably fast and reasonably light. They are less suitable for off-road use, speed or long distance riding.

Racing: Light frames, narrow tires and handlebars that curve forwards are all characteristic of this type of bike. They are fast but unusable on rougher terrain. They typically have higher gearing allowing greater speeds on the flat or downhill.

Rickshaw bicycles: Often seen outside train stations in London and commonly on the streets of Amsterdam, these are capable of taking a passenger or carrying a much larger cargo than other bikes. They do not have a high top speed and do not cope well with rougher conditions.

Recumbent bicycles. On these, the rider is in a more or less horizontal position. They come in 2 and 3 wheel variants with the latter being easier to ride. The position of the rider creates much less drag and so they are well suited to longer journeys. They are also generally faster when moving than most upright bikes but they can be slower to start moving. That is a concern when the bike may be used to escape zombies.

Electric bicycles: More properly, these are electrically assisted pedal bikes. Given that electricity is likely to be unavailable unless and until you have a base of operations with an independent supply (see chapter 11), the electric motor and gearing are likely to be a useless weight. It is unlikely that this will prove to be a useful choice in the short term.

Motorcycles

These have many of the advantages of bicycles in that they can go almost anywhere and can outrun zombies. However, they are noisy and require fuel although by comparison with cars, not much fuel. Larger American motorcycles are the most "thirsty" (barely cheaper than a saloon car) while some of the smaller Japanese bikes can manage more than 130 MPG. They are typically very much faster than bicycles. This could reduce the impact of the noise since zombies may hear you but if you are going through their area at 50 MPH, it is unlikely that they will pose much threat to you. Motorcycles provide very little protection for the rider although some types have fairings (bodywork) that offers some shielding from wind and the elements. Because of the higher speeds, falling off a motorcycle is likely to result in significant injuries and protective gear is strongly recommended. It is important to recognise that roads will be unmaintained after Z-day and debris is to be expected.

There are a number of types of motorcycle:

Moped: These are small motorcycles with a top speed of 31 MPH (limited by settings within the engine) and typically very little cargo capacity. While better than walking, they offer no real advantage over bicycles and are noisy without having the ability to easily outrun Sprinters since acceleration is generally low. They have very limited off road ability.

Scooters: Some of these are limited in the same way as mopeds while some have larger engines and a more respectable top speed and better acceleration. They are characterised by being of a "step through" design where there is a floor, fairings and a seat. The Vespa range is typical of scooters. The lower centre of gravity makes the scooter more stable than some other motorcycles and the small wheels and short wheelbase give a small turning circle. There is typically a small cargo area under the seat. While these are more comfortable than some other bikes, they are not typically well suited to long distance travel although some of the larger (and rarer) types could be suitable. The smaller wheels are a drawback in rough terrain.

Roadsters (stock motorcycles): These range in power from the relatively humble 125 CC engine powered bikes intended for learners and with a top speed in the range of 80 MPH with a single rider to road legal sports bikes with a top speed in excess of 170 MPH. They can be equipped with panniers and/or a top box (mounted high at the rear) to increase cargo capacity. They are relatively difficult to ride and the larger models are overpowered for the sort of use needed in a post-apocalypse Britain. They are noisy but nothing is likely to catch up with you if you are able to ride them at speed. The smoother tyres make them less suitable for off road use and heavy loading will adversely affect handling especially where top boxes are used.

Motocross bikes: There are a range of street legal motocross type motorcycles. While the legality of them is of limited concern, this means that they will have headlights and other useful features that are less likely to appear on a sports bike due to weight concerns. Typically they will have engines in the 125-250CC range and tires suitable for off-road use. There are also a larger number of non-road legal bikes of this type. They typically have no cargo capacity which rather limits their usefulness.

Tadpole type trike

Trikes and bikes with sidecars: Trikes have 3 wheels, with two parallel wheels at the back being the most common design. A bike with a sidecar has a pod bolted to the side of the bike and an extra wheel on the pod. In the UK, the sidecar fits on the right hand side of the bike. The sidecar will affect the handling of the bike since there is additional drag on that side. This is most notable during braking. Trikes do not have this issue. Because the additional wheel, trike do not fall over when you stop or ride slowly. However, they can tip if the rider attempts to corner at speed. Motorcycles with sidecars can take up to two passengers (at the cost of some performance) or a fair amount of cargo. Trikes often have a storage area behind the pair of wheels at the back (tadpole type) or front (delta type).

While trikes are less manoeuvrable, they may be more suitable if you have less experience with motorcycles. They are not especially common. Because of the additional weight and drag, they are rather slower than a normal motorcycle with the same sized engine.

Quadbikes: These are all terrain vehicles and a staple of modern farm life. They appear more stable than motorcycles and at low speed, this is the case. However, at higher speeds, they have a tendency to tip, often rolling on to the rider. While wider than a motorcycle, they can get to most places where a person could walk. There are limited options for cargo although trailers can be found that will fit a Quadbike. These bikes tend to have gearing biased towards the low end with a top speed of around 50 MPH. When setting up a permanent base, these will prove useful for hauling lumber and other loads as well as for transport.

Cars, vans and lorries

I assume that you are familiar with the various types of car and car like vehicles. There are a few choices to consider.

The first factor is whether the vehicle can be used in the conditions that you find yourself. A lorry can carry vast amounts of supplies but it is a liability on roads choked with abandoned vehicles. A camper van will offer a considerable level of comfort but is similarly unsuitable for rough terrain or blocked roads

The second factor is whether you can get enough fuel to keep the vehicle running. As the electrical system fails, petrol stations will no longer pump fuel. Petrol has a limited shelf life. The volatile elements evaporate and fuel will deteriorate even in a closed container. Diesel also deteriorates and some bacteria can grow in that environment so there is a limit to how long fuel supplies will last even if they are not used up. Some supplies will spoil faster than others as the shelf life of fuels can be improved with preservatives and bactericides. To get fuel from underground storage tanks, you will need a pump operated by hand or foot (which is slow and leaves you exposed to danger for a time) or from a portable power source. If you have a generator (which will require a truck to move), it is possible to isolate a petrol station from the grid and power it from the generator. There is an electrical isolator switch for the pumps on the forecourt and the wires should be traceable from there. Vehicles that require a lot of fuel will need to be refuelled more often and this is time consuming and potentially risky so fuel economy is likely to be an issue. One additional factor to consider is that diesel vehicles can run on a wider range of fuel including cooking oil. It is often necessary to mix in some more volatile fuels to thin the oil although used chip oil typically works well. Diesel engines will typically go further on a tank of fuel than a petrol car. In optimal conditions, a 1.8 litre diesel car can manage in excess of 65 MPG.

The third factor is the level of protection that the vehicle offers. A city car is likely to offer good fuel economy and it is relatively small and thus able to get past many obstructions but it is unlikely to fare well in a high speed collision with a zombie. While it might be your dream to drive a Porsche 911, they are unfortunately not the most practical vehicles even when there is no zombie threat to consider. SUVs appear rugged but are typically not as robust as might be imagined.

The army and the police force have had to balance these equations when purchasing vehicles for war zones and riot duty. They have standardised on 4 wheel drive vehicles, either modified vans or Landrover type vehicles such as the standard British army "snatch" vehicles. While these have earned a poor reputation due to their vulnerability to IEDs (improvised explosive devices) they offer excellent protection against zombies, good cross country performance and a considerable amount of space for passengers, equipment and supplies. The Landrover is also relatively easy to maintain and repair when compared to more modern vehicles. It is possible that, given that the army and police will have suffered heavy losses in the early days of the apocalypse, that one or more of these vehicles may be available. If not then it is possible, given time and access to welding equipment, to ruggedize a civilian vehicle. The first priority should be protecting all glass with metal mesh and suitable wire grids should be available in most home improvement stores. The second priority should be weaponising the front of the vehicle with heavy bars making it more suitable for running down zombies and nudging vehicles out of the way. The ideal vehicle would also have a winch allowing it to be used to move other vehicles or to drag trees or other construction materials as required. It should be noted that these vehicles use a great deal of fuel.

Quick tip: Starting a vehicle without the required keys varies between relatively simple to very difficult depending on the type. More modern vehicles and more expensive vehicles have immobilisers that disable the ignition and sometimes other systems unless the correct key or keycard or fob is used. Corpses should only be searched for vehicle keys if you are certain that they are not infected with the pathogen that causes the outbreak. It is likely that there will be many vehicles abandoned with keys still in the ignition.

If there is no immobiliser, the vehicle can be hotwired from the ignition where the key would normally be inserted. The key is essentially a multiple switch that requires a key to turn. There are essentially two circuits that you are interested in. The first is the battery switch that connects the battery circuit. The second is the starter motor circuit. What you want to do is short the connection so that the battery circuit is on and then short the wires that complete the starter motor circuit. When the car starts, you disconnect the starter motor wires. Most commonly, the battery wire is red and the starter motor wire is brown. You can pull the ignition switch out with a flat bladed screwdriver. Alternatively, a drill bit can be used to destroy the pins that are used to prevent the lock from turning unless the correct key is inserted. Once these are destroyed, the ignition can be operated with a flat bladed screwdriver. It is also sometimes possible to simply force the lock with (again) a screwdriver, breaking the pins. If the vehicle is fitted with an immobiliser, it is both difficult and complex to bypass this especially since this is often integrated into the engine management unit. It is unlikely that you will be able to salvage this type of vehicle without the correct keys.

Farm equipment

While not especially useful for general transport purposes, it is possible to modify farm machinery to be effective against zombies. While not the intended use, a combine harvester will do massive damage to a large group of zombies. With some welding, chains can be added to the combine head (the rotating part at the front) to create a makeshift flail tank. This type of tank was designed for mine clearance and the rapidly rotating chains would destroy anything in front of the tank or buried in the ground immediately in front of the tank. Against soft targets such as zombies, this would clearly be highly effective. There are also combine heads which feature cutting blades with adjustable height. While these are not adjustable to head height, it may still prove valuable as a weapon against large groups. It would be necessary to add plates to deflect body fluids and parts from entering the cab and vents would need to be blocked. The driver also would need the best biological protection that could be devised. Please see the chapter on infection control for details.

Public transport

While public transport will not be running after Z-day, the vehicles will still exist. Road vehicles such as busses and coaches can form both transport and makeshift living quarters. However, any sort of obstruction or even some country lanes would present a major challenge and the amount of fuel required to keep a vehicle of that size on the road is problematic. Most trains are electrically powered, running off the third rail. Power will fail fairly quickly after Z-day and these will be unusable. The remaining diesel trains will still run but it would be necessary to travel slowly to avoid derailments and points will need to be manually switched. At a crawl, cars and other obstructions can be shunted off the line. The fuel consumption will, of course, be impractical. Steam trains, while not common, will at least be easy to fuel. However, they will only be of use if you want to go where the rails take you. In an established settlement, a steam train could be modified to work as a stationary engine providing power for milling or sawing.

Animals

Until the 1920s, animals were still the main form of transport in Britain. There are a large number of horses still in the UK, an estimated 600,000. There are a number of advantages to horses that should be considered. The first is that they can survive on renewable fuels. The second is that they can travel over a wide range of terrain, even swimming in water if need be. The third is that they do not require a factory to replace them since they take care of that themselves - if you can find a stallion. However, most horses are not suitable for the potential uses that we would have for them. Ponies are too small for most people to ride although they can pull wagons or sleds. Cobs and heavy hunters are robust and powerful but are unlikely to react at all well to any kind of threat as it is the nature of a horse to run from danger. Heavy horses are often more placid and immensely strong although they are not especially fast. While horses can be trained to be an asset in a fight (as the war horses called destriers ridden by knights were), this is a long term project. Horses also require a significant amount of care and eat a remarkable amount of food. However, in the long term, they are likely to be the most significant form of transport and it is worth considering the merit of procuring a breeding pair when setting up a long term base. There is a final advantage that horses have over other vehicles. Unlike an APC, horses can be eaten.

While Oxen used to be popular in farming, they are now so rare that it is unlikely that you will have access to any. Cattle can be used to perform some tasks such as ploughing or dragging a load. However, they are not useful as riding animals. Donkeys and mules are typically too small to ride but could be useful as pack animals.

Water vehicles

While it might seem that these are only useful if you are in a coastal location, there are over 2000 miles of waterways in the UK not counting rivers. Roughly 50% of the population of the UK (pre-apocalypse) lives within 5 miles of a canal. Rivers, of course, run to the sea so it is possible to get to the coast from any river with a suitable boat or other vessel.

Britain being an island, boats and ships are one way of getting out of the country with the other being aircraft. If you have reason to believe that other countries are less affected or unaffected by zombies, boats and the waterways are your best bet for getting to a safe haven.

Sprinters are unlikely to attack a boat and boats typically make little noise, especially when they are not running an engine and simply moving on the current. Shamblers may not notice the vessel at all. While we do not know if Sprinters can swim, it is likely that they cannot. They still require air so they are much less likely to be in the water and so present much less of a threat than when travelling over land.

Shamblers cannot drown but they also are unlikely to float unless the gasses of decomposition have made them buoyant. Floating zombies will probably make little progress in the water and so may not be a threat – and will sink if punctured. Shamblers may walk across the bed of a river or canal. However, if there are no ropes or similar handholds dangling into the water then it is unlikely that they could climb aboard. It should be possible to discourage the more persistent with a boat hook.

Common types of water vessel include:

Barges: Normally found on canals and rivers, these are typically rented to holiday makers and the cargo space will have been converted to living quarters. As a result, this is a rather more comfortable vessel than might otherwise be expected. Barges typically do very poorly in rough seas. Vessels of this type typically have inboard motors; the engine is within the boat as opposed to external (outboard) motors. Houseboats are essentially similar. Like any dwelling, you should be aware that they may contain zombies.

Motorboats: These are often found on larger rivers such as the Thames and will typically have a smaller cabin and may have inboard or outboard engines. They are often outfitted to a high level of luxury and are, prior to the apocalypse, a rich man's plaything. Most will be easily able to cross the channel or the Irish Sea.

Powerboats: Typically powered by a large single outboard motor, these are often largely open with a small cabin or just a partially sheltered area behind a screen. They are fast but offer little protection and are not especially suitable for longer journeys. RIBs (Rigid Inflatable Boats) are similar but have inflatable hulls as the name suggests.

Dinghies and ship's boats: These are small vessels with lower powered engines or oars. They are used to travel short distances. In the case of a dingy, this could be around an area of water such as a lake or bay. In the case of a ship's boat, this would be from a larger ship to the shore and the boat would be stored aboard the ship when not in use or anchored by the shore.

Yacht: These are recreational boats that may be powered by engines or sail or a combination of the two. It takes a considerable amount of training and skill to use sails and, where possible, this should be avoided if you do not have the training.

Waterbikes: These are small open vessels where the rider sits on a seat above the water. They offer no shelter and are likely to struggle in any sea conditions other than flat calm. They have no cargo capacity to speak of. They have Inboard motors. They are capable of reaching offshore islands or crossing the channel but they have limited range. There are also pedal driven waterbikes but they are of no practical use to us.

Trawlers: These are large boats or small ships used for fishing. They have a long range and it is expected that they will be at sea for several days. The smaller trawlers can be operated with a crew of 1-2 people while larger ships require more crew. While not stylish, you are guaranteed not to starve on one of these although scurvy may become an issue.

Tugs and pilots: These are smaller vessels with outsize engines designed to move larger ships. There are harbour tugs (shorter and intended for use within a bay) and ocean going tugs. Either is capable of longer journeys. Tugs typically have fire monitors, a type of water cannon used for fire suppression. It could be used as a non-lethal weapon if needed. They are designed to have a crew of around 5 people but could be operated with fewer with less efficiency.

Large ships, container ships, liners: These are unlikely to be practical forms of transport although container ships and cargo ships may contain useful supplies. Liners are potentially dangerous as they typically carry a large number of passengers and infections have historically spread rapidly through the population of such ships.

Quick tip: Typically, the steering on ships and boats is reversed. The wheel or tiller directs the rudder and the rudder turns the ship away from the direction that rudder has been turned towards. You can think of it as directing a jet of water caused by the movement of the ship. Deflecting the jet left will turn the ship right. Ships will continue to turn in the direction that the rudder is pushing them so control movements should be cancelled out by an opposite movement and this should be done earlier than would seem intuitive. Small corrections work best. Rapid movement of the tiller will cause the boat or ship to heel around (turn) and this will be much more rapid with smaller craft. This can cause the vessel to capsize if done too rapidly. Ships and boats typically carry distress flares. There are various types, some of which are held in the hand and burn brightly and some of which fire flares into the air with a parachute. The latter are referred to as rocket flares. There may be a flare gun that the fires parachute flares several hundred feet into the air. While not intended as a weapon, it could be used offensively. Alternatively, if the outbreak is limited, these could be used to call for help.

Aircraft

It is said that aircraft are difficult to fly. This is not entirely true. Taking off can be dangerous. Landing is difficult and dangerous for anyone but an experienced pilot. However, flying itself is not especially challenging. There are over 1800 airfields and airports in the UK. There are thousands of light aircraft in the UK. Typically, the aircraft at airfields are smaller with the Cesna range of light aircraft being popular workhorses. There will also be a range of microlight aircraft, some of which such as the Skyranger able to take a pilot and a passenger. All civilian aircraft can be operated with a single pilot. Light aircraft typically take normal petrol although microlight aircraft that use two-stroke engines (typically motorcycle engines repurposed) will require oil added to the fuel. There is a saying among pilots that the only time that you can have too much fuel is when you are on fire.

If you plan to use an aircraft to escape, you would be well advised to take some flying lessons or at least spend some time with a flight simulator. I would strongly advise against trying to fly a plane without training unless there are no other options. For completeness, basic instructions are given in the section below.

All aircraft are equipped with radios that operate on the band reserved for aircraft (108 Mhz to 135 Mhz) and there are multiple channels within that band. Listening for traffic on those bands will tell you if there are any aircraft operating in the area or any operational control. Any such transmissions will be from someone who is relatively safe and who has access to power and fuel. These are clearly people that can help you. The channel used for emergency broadcasts is known as "guard" and is 121.5 MHz. Shouting for help on this channel will get you attention if there is anyone still listening. The radios are single duplex. You press the button and speak and release the button and listen.

Quick tips: While aircraft are more complex than cars, the controls are still fairly simple. Light aircraft have an ignition system much like cars. The positions are Off, Left, Right, Both and Start. You move the ignition from Off to Start for ignition and to Both after this. On many light aircraft, it is necessary to manually swing the prop to start the engine and this requires a fair bit of effort, especially for larger engines or those with a high compression ratio. The prop normally turns clockwise and it is essential to keep your hands out of the way of the prop once the engine starts. Brakes (if fitted) or chocks (wedges in front of the wheels) should be used to prevent the aircraft moving when the engine starts. The throttle will typically need to be about 25% open for starting. The throttle is used to increase or decrease prop speed. What is not obvious is that the prop speed is the main factor that determines altitude. The more power you give it, the faster the plane moves and the more lift it generates which slows the plane. As a rule of thumb, use the throttle to control the altitude and the flaps to control the speed; I know that this seems counter-intuitive. If the plane is moving more slowly than a certain speed, it will be unable to fly – this is called the stall speed. This will be marked on the air speed indicator and will be different for each model. There will be a different stall speed depending on whether the flaps are extended; these are extensions to the wing that give more lift at the cost of creating more drag and slowing the plane. Extended flaps enable the plane to fly at lower speeds but will use excessive fuel if left extended. Some microlight aircraft do not have flaps.

The rudder is used to steer on the ground. The rudder and the stick are used together to steer in the air as described below.

To take off, extend flaps (if fitted) and open the throttle fully. When the airspeed (which will be different to ground speed if there is wind) is greater than the stall speed, pull back on the stick to raise the nose. Doing so WILL drop the airspeed and so this should be done gradually unless the plane has a lot of power. The stick should be in a neutral position unless turning or taking off – if the stick needs to be in a different position in normal flight then the trim is probably off as a result of uneven loading. If the plane is pitching forward or backward with the stick in a neutral position, it may be necessary to adjust the trim wheel. The trim wheel is normally inverted (it turns the opposite way to what you would expect) and it is normally mounted in such a way that it is in-line with the body of the aircraft. There may also be a rudder trim wheel that is mounted at 90 degrees to the body of the plane. This is used to counter a tendency for the plane to turn.

Turning the plane is done with both the stick (controlled by the hands, obviously) and the rudder which is controlled with the feet. To make a turn, move the stick and the rudder in the same direction. You should start correcting the turn with an opposite movement before it is complete or you will overshoot. There is a compass on all planes and many have GPS systems.

Be aware that winds can deflect the aircraft and you may need to repeatedly adjust the heading to allow for this. The rudder and the stick can be moved in opposite directions to move the plane diagonally which you are unlikely to need to do unless there is a significant crosswind. While cruising, remain fairly high as altitude gives you time to do things.

Light aircraft do not typically have air brakes.

To land, slow the plane and lose height. Do not push the nose down but flatten the attitude of the plane to prevent stalling. Extend flaps as the speed and height reduce to prevent the plane from stalling. Ideally, an airfield is the best place to land as it has a long flat runway but any flat area will do. Be aware that fields look flatter than they are from the air. An abandoned motorway may be a good choice if no airfield is available. When you are close to the ground (less than 15 feet), raise the nose a little which will drop the air speed – this is called flaring. You will descend and the wheels will touch the ground. The plane should only be slightly nose up at this point. If you judged the height well then the wheels they will touch relatively gently. Reduce the throttle to the minimum and use the brakes (if fitted) to stop the forward motion of the plane.

When the plane stops, I recommend getting out and kissing the ground if you have made a successful flight using only this guide.

Where to go?

This is a question that is impossible to answer ahead of time since we cannot know with certainty prior to the outbreak what areas will be both relatively safe from zombies and suitable for survival; the two are not the same since, for example, the top of Ben Nevis offers great safety from zombies but is cold, barren and, in winter, can kill you. While you will have to make the decisions based on what you can find out about your new environment, there are some things that we can consider ahead of time.

The zombie outbreak may be limited to the UK in which case continental Europe or Ireland will be obvious destinations. Even if it is affected by the zombie outbreak, Ireland may still be a good choice of destination since the population density is less than 75 people per square KM while the population density of the UK is above 255 people per square KM. The lower population density will have slowed the spread of infection significantly and the more rural nature of the country will have enabled the population to survive the loss of cities much more easily than would be the case in England. The best way to determine the status of other countries is to listen to the radio. Analogue FM radio can carry a remarkable distance as it will bounce off the upper layers of the atmosphere. A small battery or clockwork powered radio is accordingly an item that you should look for as a priority before choosing a destination. Most vehicles will have radios built in to them and it is worth scanning through the frequencies as you travel.

If other countries are as badly affected as the UK, you are probably best advised to remain in the country and avoid population centres except for well-defined and prepared foraging raids. However, there are some locations that are possible (and literal) islands of safety. The British Isles are aptly named and there are a number of offshore islands that may have remained uninfected. The Isle of Wight is probably too close to shore to have avoided the infection of the mainland but it is a possibility. Jersey and Guernsey may have fared better. The Isle of Man (while a self-governing dependency) is far enough from the British and Irish coasts to have potentially avoided infection although it has a fairly high population density and few ways to leave so an outbreak here is likely to be serious. The islands off the Scottish coast may be safe havens as may some or all of the Outer Hebrides. Many of these islands are unpopulated although they could support a smaller colony. Accordingly, they would represent exceptional safety so we must consider whether they represent a survivable location.

Some have abandoned buildings that could be used as a base of operations and fish and seabirds would be a likely source of food. Most of the islands are too small and too hilly to reliably land a plane on and so a larger boat or small ship would be needed for transport. The seas in that area are frequently rough and the harbours on these islands are basic at best. However, people have lived here and we can assume that they could again.

Castles might seem like an obvious choice. They are designed to be defendable. They will have a water supply. They were built near land that could support them with food. However, very few castles are in a defendable state. Walls have fallen through the depredations of time or war. Wells will have fallen into disuse. Land will have been built on. While there are a few fortified houses or castles that are still in good condition, they tend to be in reasonably heavily populated areas. It is unlikely that any of these will prove helpful.

If you know of a location that is suitable or that you have prepared then that is an obvious destination but be aware that other survivors may have gone to that location. They may be friendly and willing to share resources and this is a good idea in survival terms. However, they may be hostile and willing to defend their location against people as well as zombies. It is probably a bad idea to try to fight for a choice location for reasons that I discuss in the chapter on dealing with other survivors. It is better to move on and find a different location, especially since defending a location is much easier than attacking one.

Navigating

The old fashioned method of a map and a compass will still work although it is important to remember that the metal frame of a vehicle is likely to interfere with a compass and it is a good idea to check the compass bearing a few steps away from the vehicle for comparison if possible. Road signs will still be present if travelling by road. However, there is a better option. GPS satellites will continue to work for a considerable time after the failure of systems on the ground. Accordingly, GPS will still be available although self-contained dedicated systems with maps on an internal data store will be much more reliable than the systems integrated into smartphones since those obtain data via the cellular network and this is unlikely to available or reliable for more than a few days after the outbreak. It is not be available in all areas even before then.

7. Infection Prevention And Control

In these days of modern medicine, it is easy to forget how readily infections of various types have spread through populations. The Bubonic plague killed around half of the population of the UK. In the First World War, more than 10 million people were killed and, of these, around half died of disease. The Spanish influenza epidemic killed as many as 50 million people and infected at least 500 million people. If you doubt that a new disease agent that we have no immunological defences against such as the zombie plague could spread through the population, these figures make sobering reading. However, there is good reason to think that the zombie plague will not be as bad as these previous plagues. In all other cases, those killed by the plague stopped moving and spreading the plague. That is not true of this new disease, this unknown agent that will cause Z-day. Here, many or most of the casualties will become carriers. This will be a good deal worse than the Spanish Flu pandemic.

Before we examine the disease agent behind the zombie plague (which I will term Agent Z for convenience), we should look at what other disease threats we are likely to face and what we can do about them. Once we have established a baseline, we will be in a better position to look at the possible specifics of Agent-Z and what we can do to protect ourselves. We need to consider the nature of infectious diseases.

While there are many internal conditions that can kill us (for example, fatty degeneration of the heart), infections come from outside of the body. They have to enter the body by one of the following means:

Ingestion

Inhalation

Contact with mucous membranes such as around the

eyes or damp skin

Wounds

All other methods are really special cases of those listed above. Malaria is spread via mosquito bites but this is a special case of a wound. Inhalation is a remarkably common vector because it gets the disease organism into a moist environment suitable for growth immediately.

Infections of the skin are astonishingly common but most are fairly harmless and some are actively beneficial – as long as they remain on the skin. Similarly, there is a wide range of bacteria in the human gut and they are necessary for human health. If the bacteria native to the skin or the gut get into a wound then they become dangerous. We live in a sea of bacteria at all times and there is no realistic way that we can ever make our environment sterile nor is this a desirable goal since some bacteria are critical to the digestion of food. There are more bacteria inside a healthy human body than there are human cells.

The main infectious agents are (in order of size) parasites (such as Bot fly larva), protozoa (such as *Trypansoma brucei* which causes sleeping sickness), bacteria (such as *Staphylococcus*

Aureus which causes boils among other things), viruses (such as influenza) and Prions (one type of which causes new variant CJD in humans). Only the larvae are visible to the naked eye. Prions are around 30 cubic nanometres, very much smaller than a red blood cell. Filtration is ineffective against such small organisms.

All can be destroyed by heat or chemical action but once inside a human body, the majority of the things that will kill them will kill human cells at least as readily. Prions have been known to survive temperatures of 500 degrees centigrade. Viruses are tough but not as tough as prions and rarely survive more than 100 degrees C. Most bacteria are killed at 65 degrees C. Protozoa and larvae are more delicate still. As a general rule, the larger and more complex the organism, the more fragile it is. There are also fungal infections that result in conditions such as athlete's foot and these are less of a problem although the broken skin is a potential route for infections into the body. Chemically, larger and more complex organisms are again less robust than simpler ones. Larvae require very specific conditions to survive and bacteria tend to be require fairly specific environments if they are to reproduce – most will not grow in a petri dish. Alcohol will kill all of these. Viruses and prions are immune to alcohol and chemicals that will damage them generally do at least as much damage to human cells. It is relatively easy to destroy these organisms outside of the human body and very hard to destroy them within the body without killing the person. Avoiding infection is clearly the best idea.

Given that these organisms are so small, it might seem almost impossible to protect against them with clothing but they do not generally appear by themselves. Bot flies lay the eggs that become larvae but we can prevent them from implanting eggs if they cannot get to skin. Bacteria can reside in materials ingested or in infected materials brought it by something that wounds us. Viruses and bacteria often spread via body fluids – saliva, blood, semen or mucus. These can be fluids that have been aerosolised by coughing, sneezing, high velocity rounds or just by breathing. While we cannot stop the virus, we can stop the fluids by barrier methods such as condoms for sexually transmitted diseases, masks to catch droplets of liquid exhaled, gloves covering exposed hands and so on. For a long time, it was thought that bacterial infections could not occur by ingestion because conditions within the stomach were considered too hostile but this proved to be incorrect. The majority of stomach ulcers and some stomach cancers are linked to infections of the bacteria *Helicobacta pylori*. Prions can certainly survive ingestion and normally infect the host in this way although there is still a great deal that we do not know about the transmission of this class of disease agents. One thing that is certain and common to all of these infections is that keeping the infectious agent out of the body is a sure way to prevent the infection.

Equipment for preventing infection

Face shield, surgical gloves and goggles. Obviously, these are all contaminated and will need to be sterilised or replaced. When removing gloves, pinch the material at the base of the glove between thumb and forefinger and peel the glove off the hand. Keep holding the glove that you have just removed and slide a finger of the other hand under the cuff of the glove. Peel off the glove so that the first glove is within the removed glove. This ensures that your skin never touches infected material.

Avoiding wounds is obviously helpful in preventing infection and the section on equipment discusses protective equipment of this type. However, there are measures that we can take to prevent the infectious agent from coming into contact with mucus membranes, lungs, eyes and small breaches in the skin. Here are some common items of PPE (personal protective equipment) that will be found in any good first aid kit, ambulance, clinic or hospital. One point to consider is that infection prevention is inevitably bidirectional. The person wearing the protection is less likely to contract diseases from others or transmit any diseases that they may have.

Gloves: Latex free gloves are often considered the best choice since some people are sensitive to latex but they do not offer the same level of protection as the more traditional type. You may think of these as surgical gloves although there are technically both surgical and exam types which provide about the same level of protection. They are thin and it is possible to perform tasks requiring considerable delicacy of touch while wearing them. They are reasonably tough although glass and metal blades can cut them and age or repeated stress can make them brittle. They may make your hands sweaty after a while which is not just unpleasant but also a potential breeding ground for bacteria. They can be worn under other gloves or more than one pair worn at a time – for example, a non-latex glove surrounded by a latex glove ("double gloving"). Where these are not available, the types of glove worn for washing up or the thin gloves sold in supermarkets for messy jobs are better than no protection at all. As discussed in the section on protective clothing, leather gloves over these would be optimal. Rings with settings should be removed before putting on gloves.

Face masks: These come in multiple types ranging from simple surgical masks to valved respirators and offer different levels of protection. Again, any protection is better than none. While viruses and prions are too small to be filtered out, they will generally be transported in droplets or other aerosolised infectious materials and these masks are effective at screening those out of inhaled air. Because infection is trapped by the mask rather than destroyed, a used mask is a potentially infectious object in itself. These are commonly found in hospitals, clinics and possibly in first aid kits. The dust masks sold in home improvement shops are of much lower quality but may still provide some protection. Unlike many of the masks designed for infection control, they are not fluid resistant. It can be difficult to breathe quickly in a mask and so running while wearing one may be a problem.

Face shields: These vary from small sheets with valves that are used to offer some protection while performing mouth to mouth resuscitation to clear masks mounted on a headband that cover the entire face, shielding the eyes, mouth and nose. A filtering face mask can be worn underneath them for additional protection and this combination offers reasonable safety from splashes and aerosolised material. As well as the obvious sources of clinics and hospitals, garden centres often have lower quality but more robust versions of these intended to protect users of power tools.

Goggles: These protect only the eyes although this is valuable given that destroying zombies is very likely to cause infectious material to be flying around in the area. These can be found in hospitals, clinics and DIY stores. Paintball masks also offer a degree of protection and are remarkably tough. They can fog up when worn or pushed up on the forehead so wearing them around the neck when they are not needed can be a better option. Anti-fog coatings are available but these tend not to last. A thin film of washing-up liquid also prevents fogging.

Gowns and overshoes: These are to protect clothing from becoming compromised. In practice, it is unlikely that you could use these in any high threat environment e.g. while actually facing zombies.

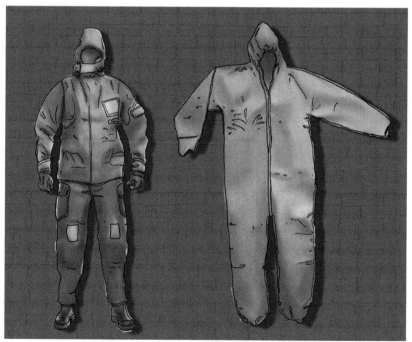

The NBC suit on the left is a NATO standard suit with activated charcoal filters and pockets. The suit on the right is a Tyvex suit suitable for use in a laboratory or similar environment.

NBC suits: Nuclear-Biological-Chemical protection suits are rather specialist items and generally available only to the military and emergency services. However, it may be possible to obtain them from military surplus stores remarkably cheaply prior to Z-day. They are apparently restricted items in the US but not in the UK. They offer physically shielding and some types offer chemical shielding in the form of activated charcoal. Military types are available in camouflage and allow considerable freedom of movement all things considered. Generally, the higher the level of protection, the more cumbersome the suit. There are also very inexpensive suits made of Tyvex that are used by the police and are essentially the same as the painters suits sold in hardware shops. These offer very limited protection but can be used with a face shield, face mask and goggles. While this will be very little use against nuclear or chemical threats, they should be used if they are the best available. However, they are white and make a fair amount of noise when worn making them something of a liability when trying to avoid being observed. They also tear fairly easily.

Essentially, anything that keeps infectious material from passing from one person to another person will help. You should be aware that after use, clothing and protective equipment may represent an infection hazard and should be disinfected or destroyed. When you have a permanent base of operations, "outside" clothing should be stored well away from the house.

Your best protection of all is washing all exposed areas of skin and drying them thoroughly as damp skin is a good growth medium for micro-organisms. Washing with a weak bleach solution or an alcohol solution is more effective than just water but will cause some skin irritation. Alcohol gels are a good way to kill bacteria on skin but do not remove dirt or kill viruses. Ordinary soap is still good.

Cleaning and disinfecting clothes and equipment

As discussed at the start of this section, organisms vary in their resistance to heat and chemical attacks. Few items of equipment are able to withstand the 500 degrees centigrade necessary to certainly destroy the most robust organisms – that is nearly 200 degrees hotter than the melting point of lead. Attempting to heat anything flammable to that temperature in air is likely to cause it to ignite; the point at which paper will start to burn in the absence of a flame is 233 degrees centigrade. Heating the object in water will cause the water to boil and it will not get hotter than 100 degrees centigrade at normal atmospheric pressure. Autoclaves and pressure cookers use very much higher pressures to achieve the necessary higher temperatures. Most plastics will melt in these conditions. Any electronics will be destroyed as the solder will become liquid.

Chemical based sterilisation is less aggressive to non-living material. Ordinary domestic bleach will destroy pretty much any organism because the active ingredient in bleach, Sodium Hypochlorite, destroys proteins. Bacteria require multiple proteins that are destroyed by bleach to reproduce. Because Sodium Hypochlorite is very reactive, it can denature the proteins in viruses and prions; prions are really a special case of proteins and are not, by most conventional definitions, alive. Pool supply shops (which are unlikely to be looted) will have large supplies of Calcium Hypochlorite (typically a solid) or Sodium Hypochlorite (typically a liquid) which will do the same job. Boots, vehicles, weapons etc. should be washed in a solution of these chemicals. If you have a permanent base, you may want to create a bath of this solution to walk through when re-entering a nominally clean area.

Most metal objects can be heated to a degree that will sterilise them. Wherever possible, anything that you interact with that has been in contact with any infectious agent should be cleaned with a bleach solution or heat including vehicles, outer clothing and weapons. The last might seem an odd item to include but it is entirely possible that you could wound yourself with your own weapon. It would be ironic to die of a self-inflicted wound in a world filled with zombies.

Cleaning and treating wounds

All wounds should be cleaned regardless of their source. This is especially important if there is reason to believe that it is likely to be infected. While bleeding should be controlled if it is life threatening, the flow of blood does tend to clean a wound and the positive pressure prevents organisms from entering the wound in some cases. Wounds can be cleaned with sterile water; boiled water is acceptable, obviously after it has cooled. A mild alcohol solution can also be used. Readers of the *Ice and Fire* series of books will know that boiled wine was a common treatment for wounds in that fictional world – this will work if it is allowed to cool. Boiling wine would just add a scald to the wound that you were trying to treat. Vinegar was also used in the past. If you followed my recommendation in the preparation section then you will have had some first aid training from one of the volunteer organisations. This is excellent preparation as far as it goes but those organisations always have a luxury that you will not have – they are providing initial aid only and there are additional facilities available to treat non-trivial injuries. After Z-day, you may be the only medical resource available.

If you did not take this advice, the following is a very brief guide treating wounds. Please understand that this is far from complete and if a trained person is available, you should defer all care to them. If Z-day has not happened and you are anywhere in England, more expert help will be available.

If the level of bleeding is dangerous to the casualty or prolonged, you can limit it by applying pressure to the wound. Ideally, this should be done with a sterile pad or gloved hand but in practice you will have to do your best and hope. If there is an impaling object, apply pressure to the sides of the wound. Raising the injury above the level of the heart (if possible) will reduce blood flow to the area and so reduce blood loss.

Clean the wound and the area around the wound. While cleaning around the wound, use disposable wipes if available and wipe away from the wound so as not to introduce infectious material into the break in the skin. The wound itself can be irrigated with clean water or other suitable sterile liquid such as canned soft drinks.

If there is an impaling object, the normal advice (and the advice that should be followed if there are still such things as hospitals with living human staff) is to leave the object in place and get the casualty to hospital. After Z-day, hospitals are likely to have been one of the first places destroyed by the apocalypse so you will have to handle whatever injuries that you find without assistance. The problems with removing an impaling object are twofold. The first is the removal of the object may cause additional damage. It is for this reason that barbed arrows would often be pushed through a limb rather than pulled out. The second is that the embedded object may be preventing further bleeding by blocking or pressing on blood vessels. If you are lucky and the object has not damaged any significant blood vessels then there may be very little bleeding when the object is removed. If a major artery has been severed then there will be a great deal of bleeding which your patient is very unlikely to survive. Applying pressure to the wound and/or holding the wound closed may help. Be aware that large quantities of blood may attract zombies and you should consider your own safety when treating others. Cleaning very deep wounds is difficult and you will simply have to do what is possible and hope.

As long as there is no foreign material in the wound, you will need to close the wound as neatly as you can. If there is foreign material in the wound, it should be removed if at all possible. Be aware that what appears to be a small object may be embedded in tissues and you may be looking at the end of an impaling object. Again, do not attempt to remove impaling objects if better medical care is available.

While you would never do this in a normal first aid situation, you may need to stitch the wound closed if it is large. A sterile needle (they are heat tolerant so a flame can be used to sterilise them) and normal sewing thread can be used if medical equipment is not available. Curved needles are generally easier to use if available and can be found in leather working kits. If it is necessary to close the wound in a hurry and move before stitching the wound, it may be possible to tape a pad over the wound. To stitch a wound, thread the needle, making a small knot so that the thread will not slip from the needle. Insert the needle at 90 degrees to the wound, near the edge of the wound. Skin is fairly thick and this may take some effort.

Ideally, use forceps or something similar to hold the needle as it reduces the risk of infection. Stitches can be individual or continuous – if they are individual, you tie each one off as you go. If continuous, you cross through the wound multiple times. The amount of thread that you will need depends on the wound. A 4 inch wound will need about 16 inches of thread. It is possible to cut off unused thread. It is not possible to tie on more thread without doing more damage when making the stitches.

The needle must pass through both sides of the laceration because the purpose is to hold the tissue together so that it can heal. The two sides of the wound should be lined up as closely as possible to where they would be if there was no injury. This can be a matter of guesswork with a ragged wound. Pass the needle and thread through the wound leaving some thread behind. This will be tied into a large knot when most of the thread has passed though the wound. The point of this knot is to prevent the thread being pulled through and instead pull the sides of the wound together. Once this is done, insert the needle from the opposite direction and pass it through the wound a little distance on, away from the edge of the wound where you started. Carefully pull the thread through until the lips of the wound are together. Do not pull too hard and be aware that in the case of a ragged wound, the lips may not meet exactly. Repeat this process of alternating stitches pulling the wound closed with each stitch until you reach a point near to the opposite edge of the wound. Tie the thread off with another large knot and cut off any excess thread since it can catch on things and tear the wound. Clean and cover the stitched wound. The needle will be contaminated but can be cleaned. Any thread that has touched the casualty should be considered contaminated and discarded.

Smaller wounds can be closed with superglue or "butterfly stitches" which are adhesive strips that can be placed over a wound to close it. These are generally available with other medical supplies but micropore tape (as found in many first aid kits) can be used instead. Butterfly stitches are paper based and may become weakened when wet from water or blood.

Some surgical wounds are stapled and these have proved effective and rapid. However, the stapler is a specialised piece of equipment, hard to find, bulky and requires a source of power. Office and carton staplers are not recommended if any other options are available.

Preventing infection of wounds is problematic at best. Prior to the discovery of the Sulphonamides and antibiotics, wounds that proved fatal were typically those that became infected rather than wounds that were immediately lethal. In a hospital, it would be normal to use wide spectrum antibiotics to treat any infection that may have entered the wound. These may be available if you have been able to forage a dispensary of some kind. Cephalosporins such as Cefalexin and Cefime are commonly used in the UK and if you find supplies of these then they are likely to be useful. It is of course illegal to obtain these without a prescription in the UK so you are unlikely to be able to get these prior to Z-day and, once again, I must stress that you should seek competent medical help if there has not been an apocalypse. Antibiotics have no effect on infective agents other than bacteria and we have no way of knowing what effect if any they will have on agent Z.

If antibiotics are not available (and sooner or later, this will be the case) then there are remedies that were used before the discovery of these drugs. Honey has been used to treat infections although the effectiveness of different types of honey varies significantly. This was used in ancient Egypt and medieval Europe with some success and it is beginning to be used once again in hospitals as it has been shown to be effective in some cases of otherwise drug resistant bacteria. One of the oldest remedies used was a poultice of mouldy bread. While many types of mould have anti-bacterial properties, some are dangerous and there is no way of selecting which mould will form on damp bread. However, the majority of the Penicillium genus produce mycotoxins that kill bacteria and they are common in the air and soil of Britain.

It is unlikely that you will be able to do much about viral infections although these are typically systemic rather than limited to a wound. Supportive care is likely to be the only option that you have. Typically, a fever will result. Keep the casualty warm and ensure that they have access to plenty of fluids. If available, aspirin can be used to reduce fever. Isolate the casualty as much as possible from uninfected people. Do not assume that someone will be immune if they have had what appears to be the same illness. Multiple infections have very similar symptoms and viruses change over time making them unrecognisable to the immune system.

Fungal infections can often be treated with salt water since fungi are typically intolerant of salt. Anti-fungal creams are available in any pharmacy although the high oil content makes them likely to spoil. However, it is very hard to do any damage with them. The best defence against fungal infections is to keep all skin clean and dry.

No effective treatment is known for prion based infections.

If a wound becomes infected and no other treatment options are available then another treatment from antiquity may prove useful. All maggots will eat dead tissue but most types will not eat living tissue. If you have a source of clean maggots then they can be introduced into a wound that has begun to mortify. The secretions of maggots inhibit the growth of many types of bacteria and so clean (stripped of dead tissue) and healthy wounds can, if the treatment is successful, be found once the maggots are removed. Clinical trials suggest that replacing maggots every two days is ideal. Dressings should prevent the maggots from leaving the wound site. They must not be allowed to develop into flies. The maggots of the green bottle fly are preferred. The difficulty comes in providing a reasonably clean supply of maggots. "Volunteer" maggots may come from flies that have fed on anything and, given that there are thousands or millions of unburied bodies and zombies, these flies could be carrying a huge range of infections. It may be possible to breed a colony under controlled conditions or you could be lucky and maggots that arrive by themselves could be carrying nothing worse than is already in the necrotic tissues. Some types of maggot (such as the already mentioned bot fly larvae) will infest living tissue and this is sometimes called flystrike or, more formerly, Myiasis. Maggots of these types must be removed with tweezers or forceps.

Greenbottle larvae. Note the ridges and placement of the eye spots.

When looking for medical supplies, it is worth considering veterinary surgeries since they typically have equipment and drugs to handle a wide range of cases, almost all of which are just as effective on humans as other animals. It is unlikely that infected individuals will have been taken there making them safer than hospitals.

Incubation period

We do not become ill the moment that a pathogen enters our bodies. The bacteria or virus or whatever agent is it must reproduce and start to significantly affect our bodies before we notice any change. Our immune systems defeat many infections every day. We become ill from those that it does not defeat in time. The larger the initial infection and the faster it replicates, the shorter the incubation period and the sooner we will experience symptoms. The more effective our immune response is, the longer the incubation period of the disease. If the immune system is able to destroy the pathogen faster than it can reproduce then we remain unaware that we were exposed to a pathogen and this is the normal course of events. By the time that we show symptoms, the pathogen is probably widespread. Some bacteria are normally present in the body and will not provoke a strong response from the immune system. Some organisms such as prions replicate slowly but provoke no response and so have a long incubation period. During this time, an individual may be infectious without showing any symptoms of the disease. It is often only in the later stages of an illness that we become aware of the risks.

Disposal of bodies

Whatever a person has died of, their body is filled with bacteria that will replicate without any controls once they are dead. They will give off gases of decomposition, largely methane, hydrogen sulphide and carbon dioxide, all of which will cause the body to bloat. The tissues will become foamy and body cavities will inflate. They will leak fluids from orifices and wounds. These fluids are full of infectious agents and, if they died of a disease, full of that organism. Human corpses represent a significant biohazard. If they died as the result of exposure to a zombie or been killed after becoming a zombie, they are likely to be a dangerous source of Agent Z.

Traditionally, we cremate or bury the dead in the UK. Burying the infectious dead will put the problem out of sight but not make it go away. Water supplies can be contaminated and soil can be poisoned. There will be thousands or millions of unburied corpses after Z-day. They will lie in homes, workplaces, streets and in bodies of water. They will attract flies and scavengers who will spread disease still further.

While we cannot hope to dispose of all of the dead, we can keep the area around us clear and so minimise the effect on the survivors in our group. At the very least, the dead should be dumped a long way from any compound where survivors live. If they are to be buried then they must be buried at some depth and well away from water sources since animals may disturb shallow graves and infection leaking from a corpse can contaminate wells or food crops. Dissolving the body in acid is unlikely to be practical which leaves cremation as the main practical alternative. To completely burn a human body requires about 100 KG of wood. Prions are known to be detectable in particulate matter from burning corpses so the smoke should not be inhaled.

If the zombies that are known include the Shambler type, bodies of fallen comrades should be damaged in ways that will prevent them from rising as zombies. Destruction of the brain should be sufficient. Tendons can also be cut preventing movement should they rise. This should be done even if you plan to cremate the body since it is possible that the corpse could reanimate prior to cremation. This will not be a pleasant task but it will be the last service that you can offer to a fellow human being. If cremation or burial is not possible (for example, a death in the field) then the corpse should at least be sufficiently damaged to prevent reanimation.

Agent Z – special considerations

I have assumed that Z-day has occurred not because of a magic spell or because of aliens or any such agency. I have assumed that it is an infectious disease. While we cannot yet know the origin of this disease, there are several possibilities that seem worthy of consideration. It could be a mutation of a previously known disease. It could be a naturally occurring but previously unknown disease. If this seems unlikely, consider that an entirely new class of disease agents was discovered in 2001. Only about 1% of bacteria can be grown in the laboratory at present and the vast majority of the study done has been given to these. We know remarkably little about the other 99%. Only about 5000 types of virus have been studied in any detail and we know that there are millions of types. We do not know how many millions and new types develop constantly. Prions were discovered within the past 20 years. About all that we can be certain of when it comes to pathogens is that there is much more that is unknown than is known.

Could Agent Z have been man-made? There are a number of nations actively involved in bio-weapons research. Of course, the claim is made by all nations that they are solely interested in learning how to defend against an attack but the records show otherwise. It is possible that Agent Z was intended to make a better soldier or to make opposing armies controllable or any of a dozen things. It could have been released as an act of war, declared or otherwise. It could have escaped in a laboratory accident. Wherever it came from, as a survivor, your job will be to deal with the aftermath.

The things that we must learn about Agent Z are:

How is it transmitted?

Does it affect only humans?

Are all humans that are infected transformed into zombies?

What are the first symptoms?

What is the incubation period?

What destroys it?

Since I am writing this before Z-day and you are (I hope) reading this in the comfort of your own home rather than in a farmhouse defended by snipers, we cannot know the actual answers but I will suggest possible answers for each of these questions in the next section.

How is Agent Z transmitted?

We can be sure that the disease is transmissible since there would need to be many, many victims before there was a failure of society so fundamental that we must talk in terms of survivors and an apocalypse. The Agent Z pathogen would have to be highly infectious. An obvious mechanism for infection would be contact with the infected, Sprinters or Shamblers. Body fluids from zombies are likely to contain high levels of Agent Z. Bites will be infectious. Scratches from fingernails are likely to be infectious. The breath of zombies may well contain aerosolised droplets containing Agent Z. Do zombies breathe? Since Sprinters would have to have life processes broadly similar to our own, we can reasonably assume that they do. Do Shamblers breathe? That is harder to know. If they can make vocal sounds, it is probably best to assume that they can breathe and their breath can be infectious.

If we assume that the body fluids of the infected are hazardous, we expose ourselves every time that we use a weapon. Bladed weapons spray body fluids when used and this is called cast off. Blood or other fluids can be splashed by blunt weapons. Guns spray tissue into the air whenever a round hits. Bombs can literally disintegrate a zombie and spread its body over a large area.

Until we know otherwise, it is most prudent to assume that any contact with fluids or tissue from an infected human or a zombie is itself infectious. Protective clothing is clearly necessary with gloves, face masks and face shields being a bare minimum.

Does Agent Z only affect humans?

This is actually 2 questions. The first is whether animals other than humans can be infected with Agent Z. The second is whether they become zombies as a result. If non-humans can become infected, they may become ill but apparently recover or they may become ill and die. If they recover, they may be carriers of the disease. This is a worst case scenario since infections could recur after the initial wave of infections is long past. As to whether they become zombies, that seems unlikely based on what we know of pathogens and parasites that can control other species. In the cases currently known, the control requires a very close genetic match between what the pathogen has evolved (or been developed) to expect and the genetic code of the victim. It is entirely possible that Agent Z will infect and kill any mammal but only humans become zombies.

Are all humans that are infected transformed into zombies?

This depends on how specific the pathogen is. It is likely that all humans are prone to infection. There is not as much genetic variety as might be imagined in the human race. All humans in all countries can be traced to one of eight mothers and all non-Africans to a single female line. Humanity came very close to extinction in the past. The zombie apocalypse may push us to that brink again. If the genetic patterns that Agent Z uses are common to all humans then all humans may be affected. If the only type of zombie is the Sprinter then only living humans will be affected. If there are both Sprinters and Shamblers or only Shamblers exist then the dead may rise. The worst case scenario is that any human, living or dead, can become a zombie unless the body is too damaged to function even as a Shambler and that would require that the brain be destroyed. The best case scenario is that only Sprinters exist and most humans simply die of the infection. While this might seem terrible and is indeed appalling, it is still the best case scenario.

It is possible that some people may be immune or partially immune to Agent Z due to differences in their genetic makeup. If so, they may be healthy and infection free or they may be immune to the effects of the pathogen but infectious. Someone who does not get infected when you would expect them to is clearly of interest. If they are immune and there are medical staff able to study their cells then they may offer hope for the future of humanity. However, if they are a carrier then they could kill everyone else that they meet.

What are the first symptoms?

If there are only Sprinters and only the living are affected, it is most likely that the first symptoms will be confusion and a fever. There may be a rash or other externally obvious symptoms. As the disease progresses, aggressive behaviour may be noted.

If there are Shamblers (either only Shamblers or both Sprinters and Shamblers) then the dead can be affected. To notice the symptoms, it will be necessary to understand what changes normally occur in a human corpse. The first obvious change is that the body starts to cool. Fluids pool in the lower parts of the body causing an effect known as lividity where the lowest parts of the body acquire a reddish-purple hue. Rigor mortis (a general stiffness) starts after around 3 hours and becomes progressively more pronounced until around 12 hours after death. This lasts for an additional 48 to 60 hours. Decay starts and most internal organs will liquefy within 30 days. Any variation from this pattern is a cause for concern. If Shamblers are seen post Z-day, it will be necessary and become normal practice to destroy the brain of any corpses.

What is the incubation period?

This is a question that can only be answered experimentally. If there is a clear and obvious link between contact with zombies and infection then the incubation period is short. If cases of infection seem to occur more or less at random then there is probably a long delay between exposure to the pathogen and the person becoming a zombie. The common cold has an incubation period of 1-2 days. Smallpox typically has an incubation period of 12 days. The incubation period for new variant CJD is unknown but it is typically years rather than days or months. People may be infectious during the incubation period. If the incubation period is long then survivors in your immediate group may be both infected and infectious. If the patterns of symptoms suggest a long incubation period then it will be necessary for survivors to consider each other to be a potential source of infection. This will, of course, have very negative effects on the long term survival of the human race.

What destroys Agent-Z?

Outside of the human body, Agent Z will probably be killed by heat or by chemical agents much like known bacteria and viruses. Within the human body, the levels of heat or chemicals required would be fatal to the human. Antibiotics may be effectively if the disease is bacterial. However, experience suggests that antibiotic resistant variants will quickly emerge. If the illness is viral, there are few effective anti-virals and the few that are known are only effective against a small number of viruses. The most commonly found anti-viral drugs are Acyclovir, Valacicloir and Famciclovir which are effective against viruses in the Herpes family (Herpes Simplex which causes cold sores on the mouth or genitals or the closely related *Herpes Zoster* that causes Measles and Shingles). These may be completely ineffective against Agent Z.

It may be that there is no practical cure for Agent Z other than the destruction of the host. This will not be something that comes naturally to us. Victims of this disease will look like people. They may be wearing the faces of people that we have known and loved. Sprinters may even be self-aware in a limited sense. How can we bear to destroy something that looks like us, something that may look like a friend or family member? It would a lie to say that it will be easy. You may wake night after night remembering when you had to destroy something that used to be a friend. The key things to remember are that they are not the people that they look like any more than a shed snakeskin is the snake. They are something that has taken your friends and family away from you. They are the stolen bodies of people that have been turned into monsters. If you are to save others and save yourself, you must understand that an infected is not a person. It is a thing that wants to steal the life of people. You have a duty and you cannot avoid it. In the back of your mind, you may wonder if there is still a glimmer of the person that used to occupy that body in there. If you do then I suggest that you ask yourself a question. If that was you in that diseased shell, forced to do horrifying things, sanity destroying things, how would you feel about someone that was trying to free you? I cannot answer the question for you but I know my answer. Someone with a bullet and the will to use it would be the best friend that I could ask for. He or she would be doing what I would do for myself if I were able. I would not want a nightmare parody of life. I would take my end as the last act of kindness. Can you decide differently?

8. Working with other survivors

The enemy does not sleep and they are many. A single person cannot always be on guard. A single person cannot protect a building. A single person cannot build defences. If we are to survive we will need to work together. Henry Ford said "Coming together is a beginning; keeping together is progress; working together is success."

In an ideal world, we would choose a team based on compatible personalities and complimentary skill sets. We would not choose to go into life and death situations with people that we do not know well and that we may not fully trust. In post-apocalypse Britain, we will be living in a world that is a very long way from ideal. We will have to work with the survivors that we meet, all of them if we can but, at the very least, some of them. Even under normal circumstances, groups often struggle to get along and the stresses of an emergency are likely to make this significantly worse. Inevitably, the survivors (including you) will be damaged by the things that they have experienced. Some or even most of them will have seen friends and family turned into monsters. They will be tired, scared and filled with adrenaline. Some of them may hostile. It will be necessary to be understanding. That doesn't mean that you necessarily need to treat people gently as sometimes being a strong leader will do more to help than soft words. Some will be much less prepared than you are; probably most of them. You may find yourself the natural leader of a group or there may be a better leader who you should follow and assist. The group dynamics may change over time and you must be flexible enough to handle this if the group is to remain coherent and functional.

Finding other survivors

Before you can work with people, you need to be in the same place as they are. The difficulty of this depends on the progress of the apocalypse.

In the early days, there will be many people. They may be doing fairly well at looking after themselves or they may be part of a panicking mass of humanity fleeing the cities. If you have prepared properly, you will not be in that panicking mass but it is possible that you are there because of an unanticipated problem. Perhaps you have done no preparation and you started reading this guide on the road. The people in this initial crush have survived the first day or days after the outbreak but they are only survivors in the most literal sense. While there are many people, you will need to decide for yourself who has the potential to be a survivor in the longer term. Gut feel will be a major factor but there are some things that may act as clues.

Let us consider a hypothetical person. Are they looking for people to tell them what to do? I am not asking if they are following a leader; the ability to follow a good leader is a survival asset. Are they looking for the police or the government or some other authority figure to give them instructions on what they need to do to make the situation go away? If so, they may lack initiative and this is not something that you necessarily want in a team member. Have they brought anything with them? If so, are they things that you would have chosen? If the items are not but you can see a good reason why they would be sensible choices then they may be someone who thinks differently than you and who has made good decisions in a hurry. That person could be a very valuable asset. On the other hand, if they have brought things that would seem like useless junk or they have taken things that have a high retail price but little utility then that is a bad sign. Are they looking for information to make decisions from or are they telling people what to do based on their personal beliefs? It is certain that there will be much that is unknown in the days following the outbreak and dogmatic beliefs are likely to be a problem. Are they holding it together? While the early days will be stressful, things will get worse before they get better.

At this point, you have the luxury of choosing who to team up with and you can decide if a person would be an asset or a liability in the days to come. In the worst case, you will team up with someone who needs more help than they can offer but that may still be better than going it alone. Even the worst partner can shout a warning and, if you are good at working with others, you may be able to help them to become more effective.

As the situation develops, the number of people will be reduced. Some will be killed by lack of preparedness, some by the foolishness of themselves or of others and some by simple bad luck. Luck is a slippery concept. Before promoting a soldier, Napoleon would ask "Is he a lucky man?" I don't think that he believed that the fates favoured one man above another as Bonaparte was very much a pragmatist. I think that he was recognising that some people succeed without there being an obvious explanation. The truth is that extraordinary results rarely come from playing the safest option and yet in the section on fighting zombies, I have urged you to take the safest options whenever possible. Some people will take silly risks and get away with it. In this specialised context, a lucky survivor is one who has survived not by good planning or sensible decisions but one who has survived despite the lack of these things. It might seem foolish that I am arguing against the wisdom of Napoleon and against success but luck runs out. Sooner or later, someone who relies on luck will get killed and he or she might take you with them. If you can, choose someone who doesn't need luck.

So, if the lucky man or woman is one of the types of survivor that you might meet, are there any other types? In reality, people rarely fall wholly into one type or another and the following descriptions are just ways of thinking about attributes of survivors.

The survivalist: This is a man (or more rarely a woman) who has waited for Z-day as a chance to be who they wanted to be. They have dreamed of living off their cunning in a place without laws. They have probably studied weapons in magazines like *Guns and Ammo*. They may see the apocalypse as a deadly serious game. It may seem that I am painting a very negative picture of this type of survivor but there is a bit of this in all of us. Many soldiers are of this mind-set – war is a game where the penalty for losing is absolute. That doesn't necessarily make them worse soldiers.

It may be that the survivalist is ex-army or wanted to join the army. He may be a little gung-ho but he might well be able to handle himself in a fight and excitement in the face of danger is better than paralysing terror. You could do worse than to team up with someone like this. Perhaps the best mix is to have someone more cautious as the buddy of the survivalist as the team could be flexible without being foolhardy.

The predator: The predator is very much out for him or herself. They will often have a lot of gear, much of which they took it off others weaker than themselves. Maybe they killed other survivors directly or maybe they just took things that would have allowed others to survive. As an individual, the predator type can survive very well; their ruthlessness can be very efficient. However, their attitude is the opposite of what you would want in a team member. They are looking out for number one. They may fall in with a group if it seems likely that the group will protect them. You might be thinking that no-one would want a person like this in a group and this is true except in one specific case. If you are that person, you want others to join you so that you can use them.

The protected: This is a person who has survived because others have put the safety of the protected above their own. They may be younger. They may be attractive. It may be that they have talents that could be useful but that they have not had a chance to show. The desire of others to protect this person may work for them as a survival strategy but it is less likely that they will be an asset to you or your team.

The shell-shocked: This is an ordinary person who is doing their best but is barely holding on to sanity. They may have useful talents and they may be an asset in the long term. In the right team, they could recover and be valuable. Alternatively, they could come unglued at a critical moment and put others in danger. If you pick up someone like this, it is best to put them in a supporting role where, if they do lose it at a critical moment, they are not doing something vital to the larger team.

The professional: This person has survived by being trained and resourceful. They may well be a survivor from the military who realised that a frontal assault on the zombies was a bad idea.

They are likely to have a good grasp of tactics. They may have a decent grasp of strategy. They are very likely to bring valuable skills to the group. Given what they bring, they may expect to be the leader and that may not be a bad idea. If they have experience of command (which will be normal for any non-commissioned officer) then they may work well in that role.

The leader: The leader is someone who inspires others. People follow him or her. They can be great at motivating a team and bringing out the best in team members. They often think in terms of goals and the strategies that will achieve those goals. A good leader is perhaps the most dangerous person to have in a team. The properties that make someone a leader are not the same as the properties that enable that person to make good decisions. A good leader who is a poor manager or a bad strategist can lead a good team into disaster.

The cautious: This person is one who measures twice and cuts once. They don't take risks that they can avoid. They have survived by looking for the least dangerous option. The biggest risk with taking on someone with this type of character is that they can get locked in analysis paralysis. However, as an advisor to a leader, as a lieutenant, this sort of person can be a great asset.

The strategist: This sort of person plans ahead. They may well have a copy of this book (available at all good stores prior to Z-day). They calculate risk versus reward. They tend to be rather academic and less action oriented. They have a tendency to be arm-chair generals. They may or may not be good leaders but they are excellent advisors for a good leader.

So, this brings us back to Sun Tzu - "It is said that if you know your enemies and know yourself, you will not be imperilled in a hundred battles; if you do not know your enemies but do know yourself, you will win one and lose one; if you do not know your enemies nor yourself, you will be imperilled in every single battle." In reality, we tend to be a mixture of the types that I have described. You should work out what elements you have within you. You should create a group that fits in with your strengths and bolsters the areas where you are weak – or join a group where you can be useful. It may be that your role is not to be the leader and that is not a bad thing. Your job is to survive and to help others to survive.

Once a group is formed, the difficult work begins. A group will probably not do well in the long term. The group needs to become a team.

What is the difference between a group and a team?

On the surface, these things seem similar. They are multiple people travelling together, eating together, and sleeping in the same place. The difference between the two is how they work together and how they interact with each other. A group of individuals may have conflicting aims. They will be thinking of how they make the situation work for them. They will be trying to survive as individuals. A team must have a united aim although different people will have different roles in achieving this goal. They will be organised according their strengths and weaknesses. No-one will be good at everything and often the key to success will be getting the right person doing the right job. A group is unstructured while a team has structure.

This organisation can be done by the leader of the team but it may be that the leader is better at "big picture" thinking and a capable second in command will be the one who plans the details. To give an example, the leader knows that you need medical supplies and has decided that a pharmacy on the edge of a town is a good compromise between risk and reward. The details of who goes in and who defends against zombies in the area and who stays with the vehicle for a fast getaway don't necessarily need to be decided by the leader as long as the second in command has support from the leader.

You may be wondering why a structured approach as I am describing it seems so similar to the way that a military team is organised. The simple answer is that it works. The military have been going into hazardous situations for years and have studied the outcomes in detail. They have developed an approach that enables them to achieve the objectives with the least risk and this is exactly what you want. How detailed the structure needs to be will depend on your team and the objectives. You may be able to get by with a loose organisation or you may need clearly defined roles. Let us work through the example of a foraging raid on a pharmacy to see how a team could work. The objective is set by the leader and it is several weeks after Z-day. Here is your team:

Tom used to work in a warehouse. He is physically powerful but his only experience with guns was playing with an air rifle as a teenager. He has fought off zombies a couple of times and can function fairly well under pressure but doesn't typically show much initiative.

Sally worked as a security guard for an IT company. She is in average physical shape. She has shown herself to be observant in the past.

Brian was a handyman and has some skill with carpentry and plumbing and electrics. He also seems to know something about locks and alarm systems and you think that he may have committed a few crimes in the past. He likes having guns but has not proven to be an especially good shot.

Sumit is 14 years old and slightly built. He has survived by being cautious and being able to run fast. He can't drive.

Candace was a teacher. She is a very detail oriented person and is the peacemaker of the team. She generally is the most organised and the best at organising others.

Harry was a fairly senior manager in a company that developed and manufactured electronic devices. He is not in physically great shape since he is in his late 50s. He always seems to be able to get the best out of people and he thinks ahead. He is the leader of the group.

They have a shotgun that they got from a farm with 18 rounds left, a rifle and 20 rounds of ammunition (left behind by a soldier who had become infected and wandered off), and a pistol with 9 rounds that they recovered from a police station. They also have a 4 x 4 which Brian has improved by adding some grills over the glass and bull bars and a family saloon car that is a tight squeeze for the whole team to fit in. They have a selection of crowbars, axes and other tools. They have 2 walkie-talkie type radios with a range of around half a mile. The team has a base in a house 8 miles from the town. This is a well-supplied and relatively successful team.

After some discussion, it is discovered that several of the team have been to the town before but not since before Z-day. No-one has detailed knowledge of the area. Candace proposes that a reconnaissance visit is needed before the raid can be planned in detail. To conserve fuel, this and the raid will be done in a single trip. The base will be secured as best possible with flags (see section on establishing a long term base) on the doors so that the team will know if anyone has entered the base while they were away.

The 4 x 4 is the best vehicle for the job. The merit of a reconnaissance visit is briefly discussed and after a while, everyone agrees. Team members are assigned to look for specific things and to look left, right, ahead and behind. Brian is to look for ways in and security systems. Sally is also looking for security systems and will advise Brian if she is familiar with that type of system. Harry will drive and watch front. Candace will watch front and left. Tom will watch front and right. Sumit will watch rear. Tom gets the rifle, Candace takes the pistol, Sally gets the shotgun and will sit in the back with Sumit. It is not expected that the weapons will be used in the reconnaissance trip as they are not practical within a vehicle and it will be better to simply drive away from trouble.

Note that everyone has a job. There are two reasons for this. The first is practical since they are more likely to see what they need to see if everyone is looking and, by assigning roles, they are less likely to miss things. The second is psychological. If everyone has a job, everyone feels part of the team. Sumit has the smallest role here but Harry takes him to one side to stress that he is the only one looking out of the rear and so he needs to keep his eyes open because it is an important job. In fact, it is the least important of the roles but Sumit will feel included and motivated and that is what Harry wants for his team.

The team puts on its best protective gear. This is discussed in more detail in the section on equipment.

The trip to the edge of town is uneventful and takes place in the morning. There are some abandoned vehicles but the 4 x 4 is able to drive around them. Harry drives slowly past the pharmacy. No zombies are visible at this time. Brian sees that the door to the pharmacy is shut and the sign reads "closed" meaning that the door is probably locked. There is an obvious burglar alarm on the wall. Sally comments that it is almost certainly a dummy. She thinks it likely that there would be a silent alarm linked to a security company. Candace sees that there is a baker's opposite that has been broken into and presumably looted. Harry notes that there has been a fire in one of the buildings to the front but there is no smoke suggesting that this happened some time ago. Sumit noticed that there is a side road that seemed to lead to a car park behind the row of shops. Candace points out that deliveries probably came in this way and there is likely to be an entrance to the rear. The team agree and Harry reverses to go into the car park.

At this point, Sumit notices that one of the parked cars to the rear contains someone. Harry brakes so that the team can have a good look but keeps looking forward and to the sides because everyone else will be looking at the car. The team looks and decides that the person in the car is dead and not a zombie or a survivor – there are obvious signs of decay and they did not react in any way to the vehicle. Harry continues to drives the 4 x 4 into the car park. There are some parked cars and a van here. Because the team's vehicle is relatively secure against zombies, Harry drives it slowly to the end of the car park rather than having the team look on foot. Brian and Sally spot the metal roll down shutter door at the rear of the pharmacy and another alarm box which Sally again thinks is a decoy. Tom spots a corpse slumped by one of the bins. It has been chewed on, apparently by rats, and is sitting in the centre of a large black stain which suggests that the person bled to death. There is a knife near the body. The team could investigate further but there is no apparent advantage to doing so and so Harry makes the call not to do so when it becomes clear that it is not going to move. Candace points out that there is an upper story that could be a flat and may contain zombies, survivors or food that is worth salvaging.

Corpses should always be checked and assumed to be shamblers until proven otherwise.

At this point, a decision needs to be made. The team probably have enough information to go ahead and make a plan. If it will take a long time to make a plan, they should get to a safer area and discuss how they will tackle this problem while not in an area that may contain multiple zombies. However, this seems reasonably straightforward and Harry makes the call. They are going to go in and they are going to go with the roles that they had discussed prior to the reconnaissance. Brian is going to get the door open then get out of the way. Sally and Tom are going in with sacks and will gather as much as they can. Rather than looking for specific medication, they are going to fill the sacks and the medicines will be sorted at the base. There is another entrance to the pharmacy at the front. It is likely to be locked but that is not certain. One of the team could go around and check it but that would put them in danger. It will be safer to check from inside once the back door is open. Candace will be going in with them and checking the lock will be her job. She will have one of the radios and Harry will have the other. Tom is taking the shotgun. Candace gives the pistol to Sumit so that there will be a weapon outside of the pharmacy and assigns him to cover the entrance to the car park.

Sumit moves to position nearer the entrance to the car park with the pistol. His job is to look and listen and alert Harry if there is any threat coming. Harry will stay with the vehicle. He has a choice to make. If he switches off the engine, it will be easier for Sumit and the team entering the building to hear any threats and it is less likely that the noise will draw zombies or survivors. However, if he switches off the ignition then there is a risk that the vehicle will not restart. It has never given any trouble before and the engine is warm. Harry decides to shut down the engine.

Brian forces the lock with some help from Tom. The roller door goes up and makes more noise than anyone would want. Everyone winces. Tom, Sally and Candace go in. Brian covers them with the rifle. The team inside the building stops to listen and look. Tom has the shotgun to his shoulder and is looking around with the others. This is a store room and contains boxes. The ones nearest are labelled and apparently contain toiletries. There is a door ahead which probably leads into the dispensary and there are stairs up to the next floor. They turn a corner and so there is poor visibility there. Candace quietly tells Brian to cover the stairs.

There is an alarm panel on the wall by the door and it is lit up, obviously powered by batteries since the national grid has been offline for weeks. Sally looks at the alarm and sees that it is expecting a disarm code. There is nothing to lose so she tries a few common codes and the defaults which she happens to know from her previous work. In this case, it is not one of the common codes and the alarm triggers after 5 attempts. There is no sound here at the pharmacy. Sally was right in thinking that it was a silent alarm linked to a security company.

Candace listens for a few seconds. She can't hear any sounds but the beeping from Sally using the alarm is not helping. However, Candace understands why Sally is doing that and it may save a lot of noise later. The beeping stops and there is no sound for a second. Brian reports that he can hear movement upstairs. He calls up the stairs, "Hello? Human and friendly down here." There is no reply and the sound continues to get closer. Tom and Brian are now both covering the stairs. Candace and Sally move to block the door into the rest of the shop and Candace radios Harry to say that there is movement. With a crash, a Shambler falls down the stairs and Brian jumps back, swearing. Tom fires at point blank range with the shotgun and blows the top of the zombie's head off. Everyone is going to have to disinfect their boots and trousers.

Candace radios Harry to let him know what has happened and says that she is going to send Brian and Tom upstairs to check if there are more zombies. Harry tells her to hold and calls quietly to Sumit and asks if there is any reaction to the sound of the shot. Sumit reports that he can't see any change and then corrects himself, saying that he can see a Sprinter down the street and it is sniffing and looking around. Harry decides that Sumit is badly exposed and the pistol is going to be nearly useless at that range. He radios Candace to tell her that he is swapping Sumit and Brian as there is a Sprinter in the street. Candace sends Brian who takes up position near the bin where Sumit was and Sumit comes in to the Pharmacy. Candace tells Sumit and Tom (the only armed people) to check upstairs and reminds them to cover each other.

At the entrance to the car park, Brian has time to aim properly and takes down the Sprinter without checking with Harry or Candace — team members need to have the ability to act independently. Harry lets Candace know that the Sprinter is dealt with. Tom and Sumit start checking upstairs leaving Candace and Sally downstairs. Given that the level of threat is likely to become greater, Candace decides to check what is behind the door and lets Harry know so that he can factor that into any decisions. He OKs this.

The door opens into the dispensary and Candace can see into the public area of the shop. She and Sally move forward, checking around corners and behind counters for zombies. They don't find any threats so Sally starts stuffing sacks. Candace remembers that she was supposed to check that the front door was locked and she does this now — it was locked. On the way back to the dispensary, she sees that there are bandages and grabs them. She leaves the door to the back open so that she will hear if Tom or Sumit shout down. Candace joins Sally in stuffing sacks. Several minutes pass. Brian doesn't spot any more zombies. Tom and Sumit come back downstairs and report that there are no more zombies upstairs. Candace checks in with Harry to find out what the situation is outside and report what has happened inside.

Since Sally and Candace have between them stripped most of the stock of the pharmacy and are now going through drawers, Candace sends Tom and Sumit upstairs again, Sumit to keep

119

watch from the upstairs windows and Tom to loot anything that looks useful especially food. After a few more minutes, Brian reports that he sees some Shamblers in the distance and Harry makes the decision that the team should leave. He radios Candace telling her to get out with what they have already got and get in the vehicle. He leaves Brian in position to continue watching until the others are in the 4 x 4 and then calls him back. By this point, Shamblers have appeared from the other direction.

With the sacks loaded into the vehicle and the team aboard, they get out of the area. There are Shamblers blocking the road in both directions but they are no match for a 4 x 4 which will need to be disinfected after this run - although that would be necessary anyway since the team will have trekked infected material into it.

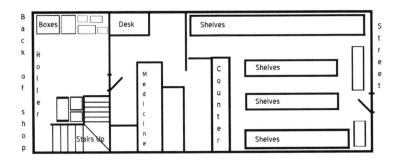

The team get back to their base, check that no-one has entered while they are away and settle down to an evening of checking through the supplies that they have gathered.

So, the point of this description was to demonstrate how a well formed team can work. Were they lucky? Not especially – they had to deal with 2 zombies and more were closing in. Were they well armed? They had 1 gun between 2. Their success was due to good leadership and good tactics. However, there was a mistake. The rifle is better at range and the pistol better for close combat. It would have been a better deployment to have initially arranged things so that the pistol went into the pharmacy and the rifle was with the person on lookout. A good leader is not necessarily one who makes no mistakes but one who can recognise when things need to be changed. The people stuffing the sacks changed because the team adapted to the new circumstances and there was a reasonable degree of autonomy. Also, they planned tactically. They kept escape routes open. Neither Sally nor Candace were armed when they went into the dispensary which was a risk but they had an open escape route if things had gone badly; they could have retreated behind the door which would have slowed up a zombie long enough to get help or get to the vehicle.

If you can get your team to work well together, you will have more success in achieving your goals and you will have to make fewer trips into dangerous places. Good team work is a keystone of survival.

Of course, not every person works well in every team. There are people that find compromise problematic and, for them, following the lead of others is a very difficult thing to do. If you have someone like that and they will not integrate then you have little choice about what to do. You must act for the good of the greatest number. If someone cannot work as part of a team, you are going to have to let them go and survive as best they can as an individual. They may come back with a new attitude or they may walk into the next zombie that they find but you can't afford to have them with you as they are.

Encounters with other groups of survivors

It may seem that there is an intrinsic conflict of interest with other groups of survivors. There is, after all, only so much of the supplies that are vital for survival. You are competing for food, weapons and places to stay. Well, it is true that there is a limited amount of these things but let us look at the numbers. The UK population is in the region of 62 million people. At a pinch, the country could feed that many people without importing food. The food stocks will spoil but there are probably fewer than 5% of the population left. There will be enough food. Guns are harder to come by. There are around 1.8 million legally held guns in civilian hands. There are estimated to be up to 4 million illegally held guns. There are at least a 100,00 guns belonging to the police and the army. If we say that is a total of 6 million guns and 5% of the population survived then that is 2 guns each. Some of these will be abroad with soldiers stationed overseas and some will be in secure armouries but, assuming that there is any form of response from the authorities, most should be deployed in the early days of the apocalypse. As for places to stay, there are millions more places than anyone needs with so few survivors. Some will be in built up areas but if there are that many people then the suburbs can be made safe. Any outbreak where the number of survivors in the millions cannot really be considered an apocalypse.

If you fight another group of survivors then some of your group will probably be killed. In the section on strategy, I explained that you should only enter a combat if there was no safer option. A cursory look at these figures tells you that there is always going to be a better option. Also, if you step back for a moment, in a world full of zombies, how could it possibly make sense to kill some of the few humans who survive?

My advice is, unless there are overwhelming reasons not to, to just avoid conflict with other groups. If they are foolish enough to want to fight other humans, they will not last long anyway. However, there are things that you will need and if they try to take them from you, you have no real option but to fight. If this happens, you will need to kill at least the leader of the other group.

A question that is harder to answer is whether you should join with another friendly group. It depends on a number of factors. If your team works well and is being successful then you may decide not fix something that is not broken. However, a larger group of people can secure more land and will be more resilient to attacks. A lot will depend on the personality and the wishes of the leaders of the two groups since it is likely that a good leader will have a team that feels a great deal of loyalty to him or her. They may not be able to work as well for a leader with a different style. However, there is certainly a potential for combined operations to achieve shared goals or reclaim valuable but otherwise unobtainable materiel. Ultimately, people will have to work together to build a new society in a very changed world. That doesn't mean that teams must merge but they have to be willing to work with each other. It may be possible or desirable to trade items and help each other out on a quid pro quo basis – something for something.

Other survivors and Agent Z

Surviving in a post apocalypse world is going to involve exposure to the infective agent that caused the outbreak.

Protecting ourselves against it needs to be a part of our everyday efforts and procedures. This was discussed in the section of infection prevention and control. However, one vector that we cannot avoid if we are going to interact with other humans is those very same humans. Anyone that we meet could be infected with Agent Z. How we deal with this threat will depend in part on the incubation period.

If the incubation period is short, it is possible to set up some quarantine procedures. If it is known that the first symptoms become visible within 2 days, a 3 day period of observation should be enough to tell you than any survivor new to your group is not infected. Of course, team members may become infected. If there is a risk that they have come into contact with the pathogen in the course of some activity, they will need to spend some time in quarantine. The more people with whom you interact, the greater the probability is that one of them is infected or will become so.

The quarantine need not be especially unpleasant. It could be as simple as requiring them to stay in a locked room for a few days with food brought and a slop bucket provided. When not eating or drinking, they should wear a face mask. While not pleasant, this confinement is certainly bearable and, as long as the need is explained, it shouldn't be too hard to get their agreement. If anyone does not agree then you may have to question whether they belong with your team. Preventing infection is key to the survival of the human race. Quarantine could be made more unpleasant by requiring the person in quarantine to wear some form of restraint but a suitably strong room should be adequate. Anything that goes into or comes out of the room during the quarantine should be considered infected and treated accordingly until proven otherwise. I am assuming that you will be all too familiar with the signs of infection by this stage.

If the incubation period is long then it simply is not practical to live in a constant state of quarantine. We will have to assume that the people that we interact with may be infected and live in a compromise between safety and practicality. We should limit contact where we can, especially exchange of body fluids. If we believe that the infection can be passed through droplets in a person's breath then wearing masks at all times may be necessary. While this may seem unreasonable now, it will seem the least of things in a world where almost everyone is dead because of an infection.

9. Equipment And Other Supplies

You may have the luxury of being able to obtain equipment before Z-day and you may be able to take at least some of it with you. Alternatively, you may have to accumulate equipment as you can, salvaging from wherever you can find it. I will be suggesting a range of equipment that you are likely to find helpful and some items that are not worth having but might initially seem like good options. The equipment is separated into categories. While weapons are equipment, they are listed in the chapter that follows this one. Believe it or not, weapons are probably not the most important items of equipment and ammunition is not the most important supply. You can run from zombies but you cannot run from hunger or cold.

If you raised an eyebrow at the word "salvaging", there is a reason that I used it. I am not afraid to call a spade a spade. However, looting is taking things indiscriminately, often things that you don't need. I do not recommend that in any way. Take only what you need. Do as little damage as you can while taking it. Do not spoil other supplies. If you can, leave the building secure. There are probably more supplies than you can take in one go and you want to save them for later. Other people may need things that you don't need. Don't loot. Do salvage.

Protective equipment

While I discussed equipment suitable for protection from infection in chapter 7, there is a great deal that you can do to protect yourself against injury. When we think of armour, we typically think of knights in metal plate armour. However, the best armour is the most suitable for the threat that you will be facing. We must consider the weapons available to zombies. They are not tool users. They do not use guns, swords or axes. They have teeth and hands and fingernails. They may be stronger than a human but it is fairly difficult to tear off a head or limbs. Their teeth and nails are no stronger than ours. Metal plates are not needed and would make a person of normal strength too slow to be much use. Lighter armour will be more suitable.

Armour (and any other equipment) that comes into contact with zombies must be considered to be potentially infected and appropriately cleaned. Some types of armour are easier to clean than others and that may be a factor in your choice but availability may be the deciding factor.

Motorcycle leathers: These are generally available as jackets and trousers for normal road usage and complete suits for racing or sports. They often have Kevlar or metal inserts at the knees and elbows and can be made of cow, pig or increasingly kangaroo leather. While they are a little restrictive, it is still possible to run and jump in them. They will provide a good barrier to infection and an excellent barrier to nails and teeth. It should be noted that the leather used here is much thicker than that used in leather clothes worn for fashion. There are synthetic materials used in some suits but these do not offer the same level of protection. They are available from specialist retailers but these may be found in any large town.

Motorcycle helmets: These come in full face and open types. It is possible to get clip on visors for the open face type but these can get dislodged in a struggle. These helmets offer excellent protection against blows to the head, especially the full face helmet. Ironically, full face helmets are often considered less safe when coming off a motorcycle as they can transfer a lot of energy to the neck in a crash causing spinal damage. However, the benefit of excellent protection against zombie attacks to the head comes at the cost of a more limited field of vision, the possibility of vision being obscured due to damage or dirt getting on the visor and a very significant loss of hearing. It would be possible to remove some of the padding in the helmet and drill holes to allow sound through but this would significantly weaken the helmet. Again, motorcycle dealers will have these.

British military helmet, new type in desert camouflage. These are light and rugged but cover less of the head than would be considered ideal.

Military helmets: Relatively little information is available about the current military issue helmets that began to be issued to troops in Afghanistan in 2009. It is clearly a composite material, possibly aramid fibre and similar to the US MICH helmet. These have proven themselves to be good protection against high calibre rounds. Older helmets offered less protection and were of a cruder construction with heavier materials going back to the original tin hat or Brodie helmet of the First World War with a broad brim and made of heavy steel. None of these helmets including the current issue offer any kind of face protection. These will be found on fallen soldiers and military surplus stores.

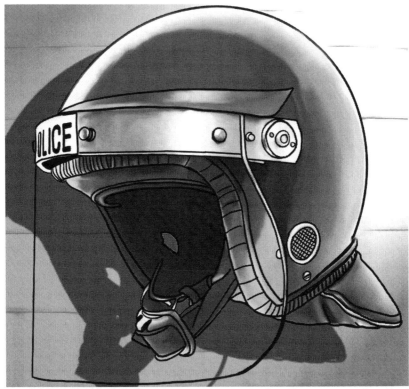

Riot helmet. Note the grillwork over the ears to allow the wearer to hear and the padded protection for the back of the neck. The hinged visor of this type will be difficult to remove but can be lifted by the wearer unless locked.

Police riot helmets: These are much less resilient to bullets but should offer excellent protection against zombies. They typically have polycarbonate face shields and cause less hearing attenuation than motorcycle helmets. They are also lighter and more comfortable to wear. You may require additional neck protection, especially at the front. Helmets of this type can be obtained from Ebay and specialist dealers prior to Z-day and from fallen police officers after Z-day. Protective gear for riot use will generally prove to be suitable for our needs since zombies are a very special case of unarmed civilians.

Motorcycle gloves: These range from unpadded nylon gloves to heavily padded and armoured gloves that offer good protection. There is inevitably a loss of feeling when wearing gloves and in the case of the more padded designs, it can be difficult to reload a gun, very difficult to reload a magazine and fairly difficult to get your finger inside a trigger guard. Accordingly, a degree of compromise is necessary here despite the hands being one of the most vulnerable areas. Availability is as per leathers and helmets.

Military/tactical gloves: These are similar to motorcycle gloves but have less protection on the fingers to allow the wearer to operate weaponry. Some types have capacitive surfaces at the finger tips to allow the user to operate touch screens. They tend to use more advanced materials such as Kevlar since cost is less of an issue. Available from military surplus stores, specialist dealers and fallen soldiers.

Heavy duty gardening gloves: Chainsaw operators and others that use powered equipment in the garden need protection from their tools and larger garden centres and specialist equipment supplies are likely to have chainmail and Kevlar enhanced gloves.

Motorcycle boots: These again offer a good level of protection. However, they are not designed to be suitable for walking long distances and they will reduce the mobility of the ankle. This is a safety feature but it can be a liability when trying to move over rough terrain and it is likely that you will need to be able to move reasonably quickly on rubble strewn floors. Accordingly, these are unlikely to be a good choice. Availability is as per leathers.

Hiking boots: These offer a reasonable amount of protection but do not come up as high as motorcycle boots. If you are wearing these with leathers then there may be a gap. They are, as the name suggests, well suited to walking long distances. Available from multiple sources. Hiking gaiters are also available. These are tough cloth wraps for the lower leg that will provide a degree of protection from bites, weather and splatter contamination.

Military boots: Military boots are similar to hiking boots but are rather higher and offer more protection at the side and top. The brown military boots issued to forces in 2012 are a significant improvement over previous models. While British army boots used to be considered to be very poor quality, the bad reputation has lingered long after the problem was solved. Available from specialist dealers and military surplus (older types only).

Police boots: The police wear a range of different types of boot which vary from light low protection boots to armoured boots such as the MLA Defender Typhoon PSU. These can be bought by anyone and often security guards use them. Specialist dealers only.

Horse riding boots: These tend to be fairly supple leather and long. While these offer a good degree of biological protection, they are not especially tough. They are also awkward to walk in because of the heel design which is intended to prevent the stirrup from slipping back and the soles that are smooth so as not to drag on the stirrup. While these offer much better protection than shoes, they are not likely to be an especially practical choice. Available from tack shops prior to 7-day.

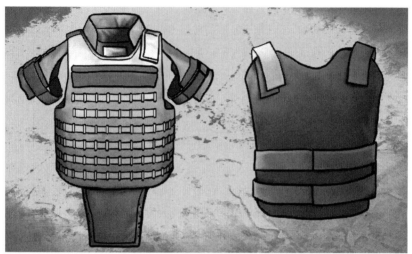

On the left is a typical military vest with a groin protector and pockets for hard plates. On the right is a civilian vest designed to offer protection from pistols and blades. The civilian variant can be worn under clothing.

Ballistic vests: These are more commonly called bullet-proof vests but they are not impossible to puncture with a bullet. They come in soft and hard variants with some types of soft vest able to be hardened by the addition of ceramic plates. In addition to being bullet resistant, they are also intended to absorb some of the force of explosions including shrapnel. While we think of these as a fairly new form of protection, there were forms of armour designed to protect against bullets as early as the late 1500s. It should be noted that hits that do not penetrate can still cause significant blunt trauma injuries and most soft vests are designed to protect against smaller calibre pistol rounds. Hard vests are able to spread the impact of rifle rounds more effectively but are quite cumbersome. More modern vests are also tested for resistance to stabbing weapons, specifically an ice pick impacting with rather more force than a human could manage. These clearly offer more than enough protection to the torso to defend against zombies but leave the arms exposed. However, there may well be a case for use of such vests if you have a team well supplied with guns but with minimal training since the vests will help to minimise so called "Blue on blue" injuries. If you expect to fight other survivors, these vests will prove invaluable. They are available from a range of specialist suppliers and (much more cheaply) Ebay. It is likely that there will be vests available from fallen soldiers after Z-day but there is a high risk of infection from such items.

Anti-stab vests: These are typically lighter than ballistic vests and offer less protection against gunfire at the lower end of the armour range. These vests range from light and concealable vests designed to be worn under clothing to bulky externally worn vests that are much the same as ballistic vests. As the name suggests, these are highly resistant to stabbing and slashing attacks making them excellent protection again teeth, fingernails and anything sharp (such as glass in rubble) that you are likely to encounter post Z-day. Again, the arms are unprotected. These are available from a number of retailers.

Horse riding body protectors: While not intended for combat use, these offer a reasonable degree of protection from blunt force trauma and limited protection against slashing and penetrating attacks. They are unlikely to be effective against firearms but would at least slow small calibre pistol rounds. They allow good freedom of movement with types covering more or less of the body depending on the type of riding that they are designed for. They offer better lower back protection than some other types of armour. They offer no protection to the arms. However, they are readily available due to the popularity of horse riding and may be found in specialised shops outside of the city and even some large supermarkets.

Arm protection: There are limited choices for protecting the arms. Military vests generally cover vital organs only. However, the nature of the zombie threat is such that even small wounds are likely to be infected with fatal consequences. There are some sleeves designed for motocross or off road cycling that offer some protection with nylon or Kevlar plates over a cloth or leather sleeve. There are also industrial protective clothing sleeves made of Kevlar and designed to protect against workplace accidents. They offer good protection against stabbing and slashing attacks but would not be especially effective against bullets. These are available from specialist dealers only.

Lower technology armour

While it is unlikely that you will be able to find armour of this type, it can be made relatively easily especially if any of your team have any leather working skills.

Padded: Normally made of linen or canvas, this armour was used by common soldiers. Typically, this was quilted and packed with wool. While it offered little protection, it was cheap, easy to make, allowed good freedom of movement and was better than nothing. The quilting adds to the strength. This offers little barrier to infectious material and is difficult to clean. When wet, this type of armour will be very uncomfortable, even less use as protection and extremely heavy.

Soft leather: This offered little protection and was essentially normal clothing made of leather. It was hard wearing and offered more resistance to damage than cloth. It would be possible for a zombie to bite through this relatively thin leather but should protect against scratches. Soft leather offers some barrier to infectious material but liquids can soak through.

Hard leather: This is typically made in one of two forms.

The first is a rigid breastplate or greaves (leg protection) or vambraces (arm protection) made of a form of hardened leather known as cuirboulli ("boiled leather"). This is a tree bark tanned leather that is dipped in water that is about as hot as your hand can stand – this is normally about 80 degrees centigrade. The leather is dipped from 2-3 minutes although the exact time will vary according to the thickness of the leather and the openness of the grain. While it is still hot and wet, it is pressed into the shape that is required and allowed to cool and dry. Alternatively, the leather is heated in a fairly cool oven to about the same temperature and painted with melted wax. The hardened leather can again be moulded into shape. This process allows quite precise shaping into a mould and both shrinks and thickens the leather. The water hardened version is more resilient to damage while the wax hardened version offers better protection against contamination.

The second form is simpler and consists of layers of hard leather plates over a softer leather body. These are anchored at the top only allowing them to slide over each which enables the wearer to bend. This offers less protection since an attack could get behind a plate (although it is still better than soft leather) and the plates can deflect blows, arrows and possibly low energy rounds, especially if they strike at an angle.

Brigandine: This is cloth or leather armour with small metal plates riveted to it or sandwiched between two layers and riveted. While heavy, this armour offers generally good protection against slashing attacks and reasonable protection against piercing attacks. It would offer some protection against low velocity bullets but it is likely that a high velocity round would push one of the plates into the body. It would provide a good level of defence against zombies. This style of armour evolved independently in several parts of the world.

Chainmail: This is composed of linked rings of metal and could be a single piece covering the head, arms and torso or separate pieces. This type of armour also evolved independently in several parts of the world. Well-made chain is practically impossible to cut through with most slashing weapons although a degree of blunt trauma could occur since the mail is flexible. Crossbow bolts and arrows could sometimes penetrate and needle thin punch-daggers were created to slip between the rings. It offers no protection against infection but is normally worn over soft leather. While meshes are sometimes a part of bullet resistant armour, chain mail by itself offers very little protection against incoming fire. The main disadvantage of this type of armour is that it is heavy although it does allow considerable freedom of movement. Butchers sometimes wear chain mail under a coat to prevent accidents while cutting. It is possible to manufacture armour of this type without access to any tools more advanced than a metal rod, some wire cutters and a pair of pliers which is a distinct advantage if you have been unable to find anything more suitable. To make chain mail of the European 4 in 1 weave:

Step 1: Wind wire of a suitable thickness and stiffness around a round metal rod wrapping it from one end to another. Large rings mean less weight but weaker mail. Thick wire means stronger mail but heavier. Small rings are more flexible but heavier for the same amount of cover. Fairly light mail should be effective against zombies.
Step 2: Use the wire cutters to cut the spiral repeatedly to

create many split rings.

Step 3: Close 4 rings using pliers and thread them on to a 5th ring. Close the 5th ring.

Step 4: Lay the rings out so that the closed links form a shape like the 4 dots on a die with a ring linking the 4 in the middle.

Step 5: Close 2 more links. Thread them onto another open ring and leave it open.

Step 6: Take the open ring and thread it through the bottom two rings of the initial shape.

Step 7: Close that ring.

If you repeat steps 5,6 and 7, you will end up growing a strip of chain mail. You can form multiple strips and join them or you can add links to the sides of this strip maintaining the same pattern. Typically, you will want smaller links where it will need to be most flexible. It would normally be worn over leather.

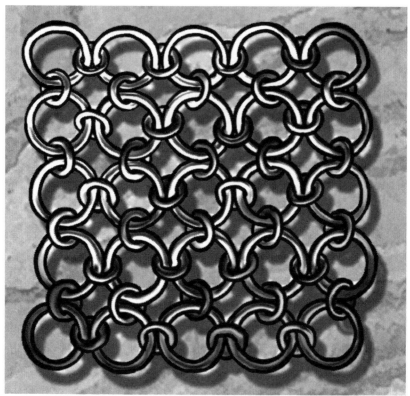

4 in 1 chainmail. Here, the rings are of different sizes giving a lighter but less flexible mail. There is a degree of trade-off between flexibility and protection since the rigidity of the mail protects the user against impact to a degree.

With decent protective gear, the threat posed by zombies is massively reduced. If they cannot reach you with hands or teeth, they are limited to bruising you or wrestling you to inflict damage. As long as any infection remains on the outside of your armour, it can be cleaned off as discussed in the section on infection prevention and control. Since guns and ammunition are likely to be in short supply, it will become increasingly likely that you will be exposed to attacks from zombies and the ability to withstand these attacks will be the difference between life and death. Accordingly, I strongly recommend wearing the best protective gear available even if it is bulky and hot. Fortunately, the British climate is much more commonly cold and wet.

Communications equipment

Shamblers do not communicate. Sprinters, if they communicate at all, will not be capable of complex communications. Humans are uniquely able as communicators. However, we require equipment if we are to communicate over distances of more than a few yards. While we can shout to be heard, these shouts can be heard by anything and could easily draw zombies to us. For range and for security, we need radios.

Multiband radio: There are a number of radios available that are portable (walkie-talkie sized) and able to receive air, marine, citizen's band and normal FM radio. While these cannot transmit, it is well worth having at least one of these with some spare batteries as it will enable you to discover where any surviving groups with radio are and detect any ships or aircraft that could take you to safety. Alternatively, it could tell you that there are no such groups in your area. While this would be much less welcome news, it will at least enable you to make plans with more confidence. Police radio and a great deal of military radio traffic are encrypted and so will not be usefully receivable with this equipment.

Two way radios: The type of radio available without a licence has an output limit of 0.5 watts. These operate at 446 Mhz and may be analogue or digital. These are, of course, incompatible. In built up areas, the range is likely to be as low as a few hundred yards while they can be usable at ranges of over a mile in open countryside. One of the very few advantages of the apocalypse will be that there will be less radio interference. Licenced walkie-talkie radios have outputs of up to 5 watts and are more specialist items. These more powerful radios have better than double the range under the same conditions. To quickly tell these types apart, low powered walkie-talkies have non-removable aerials. Earpieces and headphones are often available for these radios and a single earpiece is recommended as it will prevent noise from team members that could give away your position. Headphones are not recommended as it will be more difficult to hear things in your immediate surroundings.

Citizen's band radio: The UK Citizen's band is in the 27 MHz range and the radios are FM rather than the AM system used in the US. The range of FM CB under normal conditions is around 10 miles. These are typically vehicle mounted or home base stations – the later requiring mains power which is likely to be in short supply after Z-day. A vehicle mounted unit can, of course, be run off a 12V car battery outside of a vehicle. CB radio is no longer popular in the UK but it may be useful If you have a large group where you may have a team away in a vehicle and a team at a more permanent base or if you are running multiple vehicles.

Mobile phones: These are likely to fail shortly after Z-day as the base stations operated by the mobile phone carriers and other network infrastructure will require power.

Sensing equipment

The ability to know where zombies are is going to be critical to your survival. The main advantage that we have is our ability to reason. We can use ranged weapons which is an advantage to us. They are much tougher than uninfected humans in a hand to hand fight and they are many while we are few. We need to use intelligence to counter the threat that they pose and that word, intelligence, has two meanings. The first is the ability to reason but the second is intelligence in the military sense: Knowing what the enemy is doing.

Night vision gear: This was once very expensive and limited almost entirely to the military. Military night vision gear is still much better than the equipment that most of us can afford but there are some very good and cheap systems available. If you are foraging in a place where the military have been overrun then you may find the military versions. SA80s are commonly fitted with night sights and you can use these even if the weapon is out of ammunition. There are two basic types of gear designed to let you see in the dark. The most common is image intensifier goggles or monoculars. These cost anything from £60 to £3000. The more expensive ones give better performance but the cheap ones work remarkably well. Goggles can be worn while monoculars have to be held to the eye. The other type picks up infrared radiation, something given off by anything that is reasonably warm. Scenes which are dark in visible light are often reasonably well lit in infrared. Some systems may also have an IR illuminator which is invisible to humans (and presumably zombies) but that is picked up and shown by the night vision gear. There are also IR torches that produce a more powerful beam illuminating an area without giving away your position.

Thermal imaging gear: This picks up infrared radiation from a heat source. The display may be monochrome (typically white or green) or may be false colour with the "hotter" colours representing hotter objects or parts of objects. Perhaps surprisingly, companies that fit insulation to houses are likely to have equipment of this type although it is not especially portable. Humans and Sprinters will be obvious on this type of equipment as bright objects while Shamblers will typically be cool, possibly cooler and therefore darker than their surroundings. This gives a rapid way of telling at a distance whether approaching figures are Shamblers.

Baby monitors: The idea of a baby monitor is that it relays sound from one place to another over a short distance. Several monitors placed around a building can give a warning that something has entered the building or is trying to enter the building. Typically, cheap monitors have a single channel or 2 channels preventing interference with another monitor set to a different channel. More expensive models have 4 or more channels. Many types are battery powered making them very suitable for this use. If multi-channel monitors are available, they can be placed around an area with the receiving stations mapping to the location of the sending station giving indication of the direction of an attack.

Simple alarm circuit: One of the advantages of being part of a team is that you can have a rotating watch schedule so that people can get some sleep. However, there may be times when there is no-one available to watch and it is always a good idea to have a backup in case something happens to the person standing watch whether it an unexpected encounter with zombies or just falling asleep. The following simple circuit will sound an alarm if a something breaks a wire (indicated by the coil) which could be a switch on a door or a perimeter wire.

Thin copper wire (SWG 36 or higher)

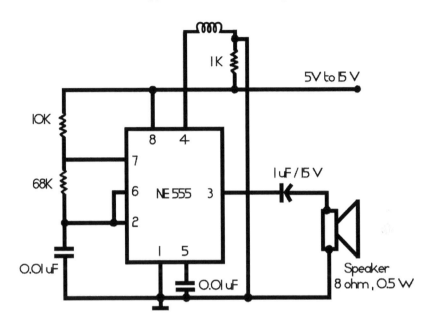

All of these parts are easy to find in any store that stocks any electronic components. The circuit can be powered by a 9 volt PP3 battery or a 12 volt car battery. While this type of alarm is suitable for use against zombies, it is simple to disable by cutting one of several wires.

If the parts or the skill required to build this are not available, hanging metal sheets over a door will make a considerable noise when someone passes through carelessly although this will give less warning than a more sophisticated wire based system.

Tools and related equipment

Lockpicks: As mentioned in the planning section, it is useful to be able to get in and out of places without leaving them insecure. There are different types of lock which require different types of pick but any kit bought in Europe will work with normal door locks. American locks require different picks. High security doors are very pick resistant.

Crowbars and bolt cutters: Sometimes you need to get in whether you can leave the place secure or not. For foraging when you are fairly sure that you will clean the place out, these can be a quick solution and a rapid entry is a contributing factor to reducing the amount of time that you are exposed to danger.

Duct tape: For hasty repairs, there are few better materials. However, Aircraft tape (also known as speed tape) is similar and much stronger; it is designed for minor repairs to aircraft and has been used to successfully patch holes in helicopter rotor blades.

WD40: Originally designed to prevent water damage to nuclear missiles, WD40 is ideal for freeing stuck locks, preventing corrosion (including corrosion on blades) and forcing water out of electrical systems that have been exposed to the elements for too long. It can also be ignited to provide a makeshift blowtorch.

Heavy duty jump leads: These allow starting of vehicles with flat batteries but can be used to connect other things to batteries, connect generators to wires to restore power to an area or to bridge broken cable. They are designed to handle up to 600 amps at 12 volts and so should be ample for most needs.

Box cutter knives: Often referred to as Stanley knives after the best known manufacturer, these small but sharp blades can be used to cut a wide range of materials including leather, cloth, card, plastic sheeting and, if need be, skin. There are typically replacement blades in the handle and they are double sided so, for the size, it is possible to get a great deal of use out of item. These can be found in home improvement stores and might be worth keeping in a "go" bag.

Cigarette lighters: The ability to make a fire can be a lifesaver. Starting a fire with two sticks or a flint and kindling or even with a bow drill is difficult at best and certainly time consuming. If you are ill or injured, the task may be beyond you. Disposable cigarette lighters are cheap, not much damaged by damp and small.

Gas powered soldering iron: In the first few years after Z-day, we will be using a fair few battery powered devices. When they break down, they will be difficult to replace and so we must repair them when possible. These small soldiering irons run off the same gas as refillable lighters. Car spares shops often stock these.

Medical supplies

Drugs and medicines have a "use by" date. After Z-day, getting fresh supplies will be impossible although more supplies of equally old drugs can be found during foraging trips. The question that must be considered is what would happen if you took medicines that were past their expiry date. Fortunately, the US military did a study of a very wide range of drugs. They discovered that nitroglycerin, insulin, tetracycline, liquid antibiotics and oil capsules (such as fish oil) deteriorated markedly once past their nominal shelf life but most drugs were still safe and effective after 15 years. Some drugs (for example, aspirin) showed no detectable deterioration over the monitored period. Obviously, this will vary according to how the drugs are stored but if kept dry and cool and not exposed to the air, it is reasonable to think that they will still be good for many years.

There are 2 books likely to be found in pharmacies that are likely to be of use to you and which should be picked up if you see them during salvage operations. The first is MIMS monthly which is a list of medicines and what they are used for, and what doses are required. The ABPI compendium is a collection of datasheets for all medicines available in the UK and is more complete but also more difficult to use.

Bandages and dressings: Dressings are for wounds larger than plasters can cover and typically have a wound pad that goes over the wound, shiny side down. Bandages without a wound pad can be used to hold a pad in place, support an injured limb or simply apply pressure. Plasters are also a good idea. Exposed wounds are subject to infection which will become a serious problem. Bandages have a shelf life but the materials that they are made of do not deteriorate significantly; cotton taken from Egyptian tombs has discoloured but is still largely unchanged after more than 2000 years. The expiry date relates to the packaging. If it seems OK when you need to use it, it probably is.

Analgesics: Paracetamol is a good general purpose treatment for pain. Aspirin is useful for reducing fever. Ibuprofen is good for reducing inflammation. In a world where doctors are rare and hospitals unavailable, these simple over the counter remedies will be precious indeed. Opiates such as Codeine and Morphine are significantly more powerful but they will reduce the ability of the user to focus or use equipment including weapons. They are also addictive and large doses will supress breathing. I would recommend considerable caution when using these medications.

Antibiotics: These are prescription drugs in the UK although many other countries sell them over the counter. There are two types of antibiotics – Bacteriocides kill bacteria while bacteriostatics prevent bacteria from multiplying. Since the body's own defence systems will destroy bacteria, this is sufficient. Bacteria are generally classed as Gram positive or Gram negative based on the presence of a certain polymer in their cell walls. Antibiotics may affect either types or both types with the latter sometimes referred to as broad spectrum antibiotics. If the nature of the infection is unknown, a broad spectrum antibiotic such as Cefotaxime may be your best option. If that is not available, trying a Gram positive and Gram negative antibiotic together may be an option although greater side effects are likely. Obviously, seek proper medical advice if there has not been a zombie apocalypse.

Antiseptics and equipment sterilisation supplies: These will be generally useful. These range from kits used to sterilise babies bottles to supplies for an autoclave to household cleaners. Brewing supplies generally come with a good quantity of these. Boiling water kills most micro-organisms but has little effect on others as documented in the section on infection prevention and control.

Water sterilisation tablets: These are of obvious use and potentially lifesaving. Water should still be filtered to remove additional contaminants.

Food and drink

Many people who have considered the problem of surviving an apocalypse have recommended stockpiling canned goods, often with a quantity of shotgun shells. Food generally has a "Best by" date or a "Use by" date. The "Use by" date is the more serious warning and often applies to meat or fish; "Best before" does not indicate that the product is in any way dangerous after that date but it may have lost some flavour or crispness. However, these dates appear to be overly pessimistic. A quick check of my own cupboards revealed a sealed container of salt with a "Use by" date several months in the past. Salt is a preservative. It is an inorganic mineral. It is already millions of years old. How can it possibly have ceased to be salt in the past few months? Canned goods are sterile because of the canning process. If they were not then they would have gone off within weeks.

Canned food from 40 years ago has proved safe to eat in numerous trials. There are exceptions; highly acid foods have damaged the cans that they were in with tomatoes and other fruit being the most commonly spoiled foods. Powdered eggs have a very limited shelf life. However, most foods were still perfectly edible years after the recommended date. Some people have expressed concerns about minerals from the container leaching into the food and possibly causing long term health problems but, given the risks of living in Britain post Z-day, this is probably not something to worry about.

If sealed, salt, sugar and baking soda should last indefinitely. Beans, pasta, dried milk and similar dried foods should remain usable and enjoyable for at least 15 years. Wheat and rice should still be perfectly edible after more than 30 years. A date palm seed was germinated after being stored for 2000 years meaning that it was not just undecayed but actually still alive. However, flour is likely to become infested with flour weevils. They are not dangerous but may be considered distasteful.

Dented cans should be avoided as they are likely to have poor seals and the damage may have introduced very small cracks. If there is reason to think that the container may have been stored in unsanitary conditions, washing the container with bleach prior to opening is recommended.

If preserved food passes the sniff test then it is likely to be edible.

While canned food may be considered to be more enjoyable, if the limit to your ability to salvage food is weight based, dried foods are the better option as they offer more nutritional value per KG although they will require a good supply of clean water for preparation.

Army ration packs are light and compact for what they contain. Here is a typical pack (menu 3)

1 x Pork Sausage & Beans
1 x Chicken Tikka
1 x Pilau Rice
1 x Vegetarian Tomato Noodle
1 x Exotic Isotonic
1 x Cherry Isotonic
1 x Raspberry Water Flavour
1 x Lemon Energy Drink
1 x Pineapple in Syrup
1 x Tabasco Red
1 x Fruit & Nut Mix
1 x Golden Oat Bar
1 x Kiwi/Passion Fruit/Apple Fruit Puree

1 x Dark Chocolate Chic Biscuit
1 x Hot Chocolate Regular
4 x Sugar
1 x Disinfectant Wipe
1 x Water Purification Tablets (6 pack)
4 x Beverage Whitener
1 x Matches Waterproof
1 x Tissues - 10 pack
1 x Boiled Sweets
1 x Re-useable Poly Bag
2 x Coffee Sticks
2 x Teabags
3 x Chewing Gum Spearmint
1 x Spoon

They are also available in Halal, Sikh and vegetarian versions.

Generally useful equipment

Backpacks: These allow you to carry significant loads while leaving the hands free. It can be difficult to get items out quickly but if you use a buddy system (recommended) then you can swap packs with your buddy and easily get to your pack on his or her back.

Water bottles: The need for water is almost always more urgent than the need for food and wounds will need to be washed and contamination removed.

Torches: Ideally, have a large torch with a small LED torch as backup. Torches such as the Maglite range also make acceptable makeshift weapons when nothing else is available. Use the large ones like a club. The smaller models can be used by holding then in your fist with your thumb over the lens. The body of the torch will stick out below the hand and can be used to focus the force of a blow. While it will not do much damage to a zombie, it is an improvement on being unarmed.

Rope: Useful for a wide range of purposes from lashing a load in place to tying up someone that you suspect may be infected.

Knife: While not useful as a weapon, it is invaluable for everyday use.

Metal mug or mess tin. Suitable for drinking from, heating food or drink or for banging when you want to make a noise.

Hexamine stove: Available in ration packs and camping stores. A hot meal or drink can help raise morale.

Generators: These are available in a range of sizes. They are powered by a petrol or more commonly a diesel motor that drives an electrical generator. They typically supply 3 to 5 Kilowatts of power and often output 12 volts (DC), 115 volt (AC) and 240 volts (AC). They range from moderately noisy to fairly loud and they are not light. Lighter units are around 500lbs in weight while a heavy unit may weigh up to 1000 lbs. They are one of very few real options for powering non-portable equipment. They are a staple of the mobile catering units found in carparks and lay-bys.

Distractors

Except when trying to clear an area that you plan to hold, you are probably best advised to avoid combat with zombies since that is risky and it is likely to use resources that are scarce. If you need to get one or more zombies out of an area for a time, a diversion is low risk and easy to use. There are several ways that this can be done.

Fireworks: These create a lot of light and noise. It is likely that zombies will head toward any source of noise as it might be a human. Fortunately, they are not critical thinkers. The biggest problem with using fireworks for this purpose is setting them so that a team member is not in the area when the zombies head in that direction. A long fuse is a practical solution to this although care must be taken to ensure that the fuse remains dry. Waxed cord is quite suitable for this purpose.

Toy (remote controlled) aircraft: Model shops will typically have many of these and they can be used to cause sound and movement well away from your current location.

Battery powered cassette and CD players: It is possible to record a period of silence followed by shouting, screaming or any other noise that is likely to be distracting to zombies. Ideally, you should have versions with 5 minutes, 15 minutes and 30 minutes of silence before the shouting begins. If one of these is planted some distance from where you intend to be, it is very likely that zombies will head toward the sound of the humans. Ideally, you should retrieve the unit after use if it has not been destroyed.

A well-supplied pair of survivors in open country with clear lines of sight. In addition to suitable protective clothing, they have close combat weapons and, by facing in different directions, have a wide angle of approach covered.

10. Weapons

Man has put more time and effort into finding new and more effective ways of killing man than any other subject. As a result, there are a huge number of types of weapon and many more variants on the basic types. I have confined myself here to weapons that you might be able to obtain or manufacture with limited equipment in the UK. I will also be covering improvised weapons that can be modified from existing equipment.

Unfortunately, a lot of nonsense has been said about weapons and Hollywood movies have led to some unfortunate misconceptions. Where possible, I have pointed out where these misconceptions are potentially dangerous to you. I have listed weapons in the order of melee weapons (used in close quarters combat), ranged weapons and finally improvised weapons in approximate order of discovery. I must point out once again that if you are in hand to hand combat with a zombie, the chance of infection is significant unless you have taken measures to protect yourself. There will be splashes of body fluids. There will be attacks against you. Where possible, it is better to avoid combat.

Rocks: The humble rock, half-brick or lump of concrete. Held in the hand, this is the easiest to obtain weapon of all and, for our purposes, one of the least useful. It lends the hand weight and hardness allowing the user to inflict a crushing blow. A large rock could crush a skull but only at arm's length and with difficulty. A broken arm or jaw will not stop a Sprinter and will have negligible effect on a Shambler. This is only a small step up from being unarmed and you will need to be very close to a zombie to use this crude weapon.

Clubs and Maces: The first clubs were crudely shaped tree branches. The earliest maces were effectively a rock on a stick. Later developments included flanged maces where the metal head had vanes sticking out from it to punch into tissue or armour and flails where there was a chain between the shaft and the head. Because of the weight and awkwardness of the weapon, it is difficult to use without a great deal of strength but it could be useful if you need to dispatch a zombie that is unable to move. They remained popular in medieval times because, unlike a sword, they do not become blunt and because chain mail (and to a lesser extent other armour types) offers little protection against them. They were more common as weapons for use from horseback. They are relatively slow since large swings are needed to build up momentum. This could leave you exposed to attacks.

Knives and daggers: The first knives were chipped flint blades or sharpened bone blades held in the hand. From there developed everything from the knives found in every cutlery drawer to the Balisong (butterfly knife) loved by martial artists to the many practical working knives such as the Bowie knife. Knives are well worth carrying for the utility value; they can shape wood, cut rope, skin animals, hack food into manageable chunks or a hundred other things. As a combat weapon, they are quite useful against humans but unfortunately much less use against zombies. They do most of their damage by causing blood loss, either internal bleeding from stab wounds or external bleeding from slashing wounds. While they can be and often are lethal, they are rarely quick killers. With proper medical care, a stab to the heart on a human is fatal less than 70% of the time. In practice, it is hard to get a blade into the heart as the ribcage offers partial protection. It is unlikely that stabbing a Sprinter in the chest will kill it quickly. Slashing the carotid artery (the main blood supply to the brain) will cause death after around 2 minutes for a human and they will be unconscious within typically 45 seconds. A Sprinter may well be more resistant but is unlikely to be able to stay fighting for more than a minute with a severed carotid. However, unless you have very good personal protection, a minute may be much too long for you.

We assume that Shamblers do not have circulation as such and so stabbing them in the heart will have little effect (if any) and severing a major artery will again be of little use. It may be possible to disable a Shambler by severing tendons in its limbs but it would be difficult to do significant damage to the skull of a Shambler with a knife; it may be possible to sever the spinal column or insert the blade through an eye to reach the brain. However, this will prove more than difficult since the Shambler will be trying to eat you while you attempt this improvised surgery. For this reason, I would strongly advise against attempting to use a knife against either type of zombie.

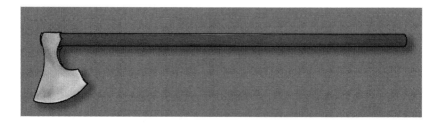

Axes: Originally a hand tool made of stone, the axe developed into a blade mounted on a wooden shaft, moving from stone to metal as it became available. We know that axes were cast from copper and then bronze and then iron. Initially, the metal axe was a tool with a narrow blade since metal was precious. Over time, the axe became specialised into the broader headed wood axe and the double bladed or bearded battle axe. The symmetrical axe of fantasy literature seems to have been rare in practice. The shaft of the axe offers a mechanical advantage and the head can be swung with much more force than can be exerted with just an arm. Axes can sever limbs or at worst render them unusable and, with considerable force and some difficulty, sever a head. Swung overarm, they could certainly break through a skull. As such, the axe represents the first weapon that we can consider to have practical use against a zombie. While less versatile in combat than a sword, the heavy head and robust blade give it some advantages. They are also common items easily found in garden centres and home improvement stores.

Swords: There have been many, many types of swords developed in the course of human history and anyone who has thought about the zombie apocalypse has considered the role that swords would have to play. They don't need fuel or ammunition. They don't make a lot of noise. They can quickly disable a zombie, not least because they can decapitate them; that is a sure fire way of rendering a zombie (or anything else) harmless. A list of the types of sword would fill a book by itself; every culture has developed at least a few. Instead, I will group them into basic categories based on how they are used and briefly discuss their utility against Sprinters and Shamblers.

Swords first appeared in the Bronze Age as a development of the dagger. Since then, they have become more and more specialised as different fighting styles developed. Some were engineered solutions to specific needs while others became sporting weapons or were modified by the dictates of fashion.

Short stabbing swords and long knives: Perhaps the best known sword of this type is the Roman Gladius with its characteristic leaf shaped blade. While it was an edged sword and could be used for slashing, it was primarily used as a stabbing weapon since penetrating wounds to the abdomen were often fatal; it would typically be held low and used to jab upwards. Similar swords were used in many other cultures such as the Saxon Seax. These were typically matched with a shield and could be used in a shield wall where warriors stood shoulder to shoulder with overlapping or locked shields that allowed a good level of protection with a reasonable offensive ability. However, while this is an effective strategy again people, it is less useful against zombies. Abdominal wounds were usually not instantly fatal. They would often kill the person hours or days later, often from peritonitis after the gut was punctured or from bleeding.

Clearly, Shamblers are not going to be affected by bleeding or peritonitis and damage to the abdomen will not significantly reduce their effectiveness. Using the weapon as a slashing weapon is also unlikely to be especially useful since there will be no pain reaction or bleeding. It is possible to sever tendons and this would at least partially immobilise a limb. It would be difficult at best to sever the head or spinal column of a Shambler with a sword of this type, especially when it is considered that the shortness of the sword means that you would be well in reach of the Shambler's arms.

Against Sprinters, this type of weapon would be more effective since they can suffer from blood loss and peritonitis and may have a level of pain response. However, wounds to the abdomen are still unlikely to quickly disable them and an attack which kills the Sprinter several hours after it has killed you is a pyrrhic victory at best. Used as a slashing weapon, this could cause enough blood loss to disable a Sprinter but again, this would not be quick and the Sprinter would be able to attack you. Accordingly, this is not an ideal weapon for this type of enemy.

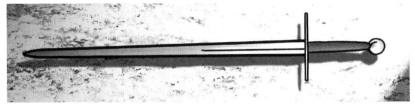

A simple one handed sword of a European type. The large pommel (the round section on the end) balances the weapon. The groove (called a fuller) makes the blade both lighter and stiffer.

One handed longer straight swords: There are hundreds of variations on this theme including the Scottish Claymore, the classic European broadsword, the Chinese Jian and the English Mortuary swords, often with a basket hilt and typically with a total length of less than 3 feet. The length of the blade makes fighting in the close order of a shield wall impractical. Instead, warriors would form a looser line and typically fight with a shield although there was a vogue for parrying daggers (sometimes in the form of sword breakers) in the renaissance and late Middle Ages. Typically they were heavier swords with an edge that was not especially sharp having two bevels coming together to form an edge. The advantage to this construction was that the edge, while not especially sharp, was more robust. Hitting any form of armour with a very sharp blade (or worse, hitting another blade) would turn the edge of a finely sharpened sword. Modern steels are tougher and zombies do not wear armour and so the bevel could be more acute and the weapon sharper if desired. Typically, there are two sharpened edges allowing slashes in either direction. The single edged Backsword was cheaper but less useful.

Typically, these swords are used for slashing attacks although they could be used to stab. The longer blade, versatility and agility of these swords make them well suited to use against zombies although they are typically heavy and require a degree of upper body strength. Slashing strokes can do considerable damage including severing limbs or beheading an opponent. Rather than relying on blood loss (as discussed, not an effective strategy against Sprinters or Shamblers), these swords cause massive trauma thus disabling an opponent rapidly. The additional reach of the longer blade allows the attacker to maintain more of a distance between him or herself and the zombie.

While no-one would enter hand to hand combat with a zombie if they had a choice, this weapon offers you the best chance that you can have. However, as noted, the weapon is heavy and extended use will prove tiring. Of course, if you are still alive to get tired while using it, you would need to be facing a very large number of zombies and surviving their attacks.

Single handed curved blades: Examples of this type are the Scimitar or Saif of the Middle East, the Indian Talwar, the Turkish Kilij and the cavalry Sabre. These have a convex curve and are sharpened on the forward edge only making them a type of backsword. They are designed for use from horseback and are not especially well suited to use on foot. The total length of the weapon could be over 3 feet and they were typically made of high quality steel (the famed Damascus steel) that retained an edge significantly better than western steel of the time with the obvious exception of the European Sabre which used inferior western steel.

Swords for one-handed or two-handed use: These are typically longer and heavier variants of the broadsword type and include the longsword, the great sword and the bastard sword. These have longer hilts that allow a second hand to be used allowing more force to be applied, both to support the larger blade and to inflict additional damage. These swords typically have lengths in excess of 3 feet and are intended almost entirely for slashing attacks. Their weight and the leverage available made successful attacks devastating if a little slow. It requires very considerable strength to use one of these blades effectively. Because attacks are somewhat slower, this type of sword would be more useful against Shamblers than Sprinters. Blows to the legs are likely to sever the leg or at least damage it sufficiently that you will be able to withdraw. Although it is somewhat difficult to strike at head height with the heavier blade, this type of blade is certainly capable of decapitation.

Thin bladed one-handed swords: These were popular around the time of the renaissance and range from the practical but specialised Poniard which was a thin blade often with a triangular section to smallswords worn for ceremonial purposes, Rapiers which were used for duelling and Épées which are used in the sport of fencing. These are all thrusting weapons that do fairly limited damage. While a Sprinter could be wounded with one of these swords, the puncture wound would have little effect on a Shambler. It should be noted that épées and foils used for sport are blunted and so are effectively useless for any other purpose.

I would like to discuss two specific types of sword in addition to the generic types described above.

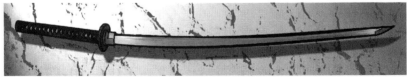

A typical mass produced Katana. There is a fuller (groove) on the back of the blade and the hilt is cloth bound. Better examples would have a ray (fish) skin hilt. There is no hamon on this blade and no patterning characteristic of folded steel meaning that this is probably a cheaply produced mild steel Katana that will not maintain an edge.

Katana: A great deal of nonsense is talked about the Japanese Katana. The name literally means "long sword". They are curved and typically between 23 and 28 inches in length. It is a backsword meaning that it has a single sharp edge and they were traditionally used by the highly trained Samurai warriors. Some popular fiction has it that the blade is of incredible sharpness. There is no doubt that they are excellent swords and the lighter blade makes them more agile than western swords of a similar length.

The traditional swords were made of multiply folded steel (up to 64,000 layers) of different types giving a combination of hardness, flexibility and the ability to hold a good edge. This was further enhanced by annealing of the edge leading to a graduated appearance of the blade known as the hamon. There are myths that the blades can withstand bullets but this has been multiply disproved as has the claim that they can cut through steel bars. Many of the Katanas found in the UK are cheap Chinese made copies that claim to be tool steel or folded steel but which are, in fact, cast mild steel that will not hold an edge.

The status of the katana in western society is partially historical since the forging was far superior to anything available prior to the industrial revolution and because Samurai warriors were excellently trained. Fiction has exaggerated the ability of these swords and associated them with the Ninja spy/assassin much loved by certain action movies. Of course, none of this is relevant to the weapon's utility in post-apocalypse Britain but it does explain the popularity of the sword. Sale of Katanas in the UK is nominally banned unless they are made using traditional techniques but the law is not well enforced. While these swords are not the weapons of myth, they are (if not mild steel copies) very well suited to the job of destroying zombies and there are thousands of these swords in the UK.

Flamberge swords: Popular fiction and possibly male psychology has created a belief in many people's minds that a larger sword is a better sword. This is simply not true. A sword too large to wield effectively is a liability. The largest swords were the German Flamberge swords (not to be confused with the later wavy edged rapier of the same name) which were sometimes seen in the medieval period. These were up to 6 feet long and had a blade that varied in thickness so as to resemble a long flame; the word Flamberge literally means "flame blade". Only 60% of the sword was actually blade with a long hilt, an elaborate crosspiece and an additional grip above the crosspiece leading to the waved blade. It would have been hard for even the strongest man to swing such a sword and, as a weapon, it resembles a boar spear more closely than it does a sword. There is very little information available about how such swords would have been used but I suspect that the main purpose of the weapon was to impress and make a statement about the owner. I do not recommend using this sword against zombies or, indeed, for any purpose at all.

A word about the care of blades – swords, being steel, are prone to rust although many knives are made of stainless steel that does not corrode under normal conditions. Other types of steel, especially high carbon steel, will rust if not protected. A thin coating of oil will preserve the blade and not reduce its usefulness in any way. Blades should always be cleaned after use, both to protect the metal and to prevent infection of the user. They should be sharpened as required to an edge that is compatible with the use intended for the blade. Blade edges can be chisel type (one side bevelled only) or two bevels that meet to form an edge. The shallower the angle, the sharper and more delicate the edge. If the blade is to be used for rough work, a tougher blade will be more useful for longer than a sharper edge where the thin metal will fold over. Blades can be sharpened with a steele (a long rod of hard steel), a diamond file or a whetstone also known as an oilstone. Whetstones often have a coarse side and a fine side. The coarse side is used for dressing a damaged blade and changing the angle of the edge while the fine side is used for improving an existing edge. Water can be used to lubricate the whetstone but fine oil will give a better edge. DIY shops will have abrasive stones of this type.

Spears: Basically a metal or stone point on the end of a pole, these are very little use against zombies because they create puncture wounds which do not rapidly disable a Sprinter and do practically no damage to a Shambler. Once an attacker is closer to you than the tip of the spear, the spear is of effectively a useless over-length pole. Ancient spearmen would drop their spears and draw a sword if an enemy got too close. One unusual feature of a spear is that the butt of the spear can be put on the ground and the weapon braced against charging opponents and this could potentially be useful against Sprinters if they attack directly – the same tactic was used when hunting boar. If this approach is used, a crosspiece should be fitted to the spear to prevent the zombie from pulling itself up the shaft to attack. Spears can also be thrown but these will be covered in the entry for javelins.

Polearms: These weapons range from pikes which are essentially very long thick spears to halberds which are axes on long poles. They are designed to be used in massed ranks against mounted opponents and are accordingly of no use to us.

Ranged weapons

The advantage of using projectile weapons against zombies is simple and compelling. They do not use ranged weapons (or typically any weapons) and so you can attack them without them attacking you. The disadvantages are that some ranged weapons are almost completely ineffective against zombies, all require a degree of skill and most require ammunition. Those that do not are ones where you throw the weapon.

When I was 10, my father gave me basic advice on gun safety (which applies equally well to everything from blowpipes to cannon) and I have never had cause to regret following it so here it is again:

1. Assume that any weapon is loaded until you have proven that it is not.
2. Do not point a weapon at anything that you are not willing to destroy.
3. Keep your finger out of the trigger guard unless you are about to fire.

As with close quarter weapons, these are listed in rough order of discovery.

Thrown rocks: Self explanatory. Unless thrown in large numbers from a catapult, mangonel or trebuchet, these are of no interest to us. It is unlikely that constructing a siege engine will be a good use of time or resources.

Thrown knives and thrown axes: While modern thrown knifes can be very precisely made and balanced, they are unlikely to do any real harm to a Sprinter and practically no harm to a Shambler. Throwing axes would do more damage and can be thrown further but are unlikely to be found in the UK and they are of limited practical use. They would also be difficult to retrieve.

Slings: The simplest sling is a leather cup with 2 cords used to hurl a stone or a cast lead sling bullet for a considerable distance with ranges in excess of 600 feet being possible. While not especially accurate, a well-cast sling stone could crush a skull or break limbs. Staff slings were also used where one of the cords was replaced with a wooden staff giving the projectile much greater speed and range – both hands were used and the staff was raised above the head and whipped forward. If you are in a position where you cannot be attacked (for example, behind a palisade) and you have a good supply of ammunition then the sling could be an effective weapon. The bullet is placed in the cup, the sling is swung overarm and the cord released at the correct point in the swing to release the bullet. Considerable practice is needed to gain accuracy.

Javelins: These are short thrown spears used in the ancient world. Several of these impaling a zombie could slow it down although the damage would not be likely to rapidly stop a Sprinter. Puncture wounds will typically have very little effect on a Shambler. It is unlikely that even an accurate hit would pierce the skull although a hit to the torso of a Sprinter could damage the heart. The blades of these weapons vary from simple points to leaf shaped blades. The maximum effective range of a javelin is around 50 feet but this can be boosted with spear throwing aids such as the Australian Woomera or the African Atlatl. These are sticks with a socket for the butt of a javelin or spear and effectively increase the length of the throwers arm giving a mechanical advantage.

Bows: There are 3 types of bow that can be found in the UK, mostly in archery clubs although there are specialist shops.

Longbows and short bows – these are simple curved bows strung with a long and non-elastic string, typically waxed linen or hemp. They may be composite (made in layers) or a single piece of wood (known as a self-bow) with the composite bows being far the better.

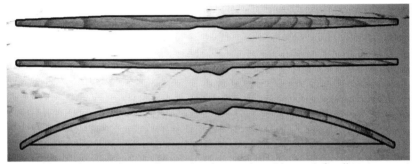

A simple self-bow shown from the front, the side and finally strung. A composite longbow would have the same shape but be made of layers of wood glued together. Sometimes horn was used for the outer (back) layer. This would be boiled in urine to soften it prior to shaping. If you ever have cause to boil animal horn in this way, I strongly recommend doing so outside as the smell is unforgettable.

The amount of force needed to pull the bow to the nose (known as the pull or draw-weight of the bow) varies. Since this affects the amount of energy stored, it also affects the final speed of the arrow. Modern bows of this class typically require 20 to 40 lbs of force to draw although medieval bows were known to have a draw-weight of up to 180 lbs. There is typically an arrow rest where the front of the arrow goes with the head in front of the bow limb (the front of the curve) and a slot in the rear of the arrow fits to the string which is typically marked with one or two metal rings which indicate the nocking point. If there is no arrow rest, the hand can be used although this is less accurate. The bow is held in the left hand (there is a grip called the riser although technically the whole centre of the bow is the riser) and held out with a stiff and slightly bent arm. The fingers of the right hand draw back the string to a point near the archer's nose with the fingers just below the nocking point. The main work of the pull is done by the trapezius muscles of the back rather than the arm. Modern arrows typically have one of the fletchings (feathers or other material) of a different colour and this points to the side with the arrow rest when the arrow is loaded. Any other arrangement will result in the arrow being deflected as it is fired. The arrow is loosed by releasing the string. Archers typically use a leather tab (basically a small leather sheet) or gloves to protect the fingers and an arm guard to prevent the string from bruising the forearm. If you are wearing suitable protection against zombies, you should not need these.

Recurve bows – these are shorter than the self-bow for the same amount of stored energy and (when not tensioned by the string) have limbs that curve in the opposite direction to the curve of the bow when it is strung. Because the bow is effectively more bent by the action of drawing, more force is available to propel the arrow. Otherwise, the bow is very similar to the standard long bow. The bow string will be touching the limbs of the bow some distance from the attachment point with this type of bow when it is strung but not drawn.

Compound bows – these have pulleys, stabilisers and other aids for the archer and as a result the pull is more even and there is less force needed when holding the bow drawn making aiming easier. The bow is more consistent to use and much more accurate as a result. However, these systems are easily damaged and difficult to repair without considerable skill and specialist equipment.

Bows can fire arrows with a range of different heads including simple points for sport shooting and the classic barbed arrow head for hunting. With practice, considerable accuracy can be obtained with a bow and consistent arrows. It is likely that a broad headed arrow could take down a Sprinter at some range if it hit the upper chest. There are records of arrows piercing skulls which makes it a possible weapon against Shamblers – although the same technique works against both humans and Sprinters of course. Medieval practice ranges (known as butts) were in excess of 220 yards long although a professional military archer of the period could hit targets at ranges as high as 400 yards. While this is considerably below the range of even a pistol round, it remarkable for what is essentially a bent bit of wood.

Bows are also practical hunting weapons and arrows that do not shatter can be reused. Unfortunately for our purposes, most arrows used in the sport of archery use a simple sharp point that is much less damaging to a target. A skilled archer can load, aim and fire in around 6 seconds.

Modern bows often have a simple type of sight known a pin sight which is adjusted for range by moving it on a curved track. When the sight is set correctly, the end of the pin (often painted an obvious colour) will roughly correspond to where the arrow will go if the bow is drawn fully to the correct draw length.

Stringing a longbow or a recurve bow is difficult for all but the lightest weights of bow unless you have a bow stringer. This is a device which will allow you to bend the bow using the muscles of your legs which are more powerful. The bow string has loops at each end and these will fit into notches on the bow. The larger loop always goes at the top. If you are unsure which side is the top, look at the arrow rest which will only work one way round. To use a bow stringer:

1. Slide the bigger loop of the string over the top limb letting it slide past the notches.
2. Attach the remaining loop of the string to the lower limb tip (in the notches).
3. Take the bow stringer. It has a saddle (or large cup) on one end and a cup on the other.
4. Slide the saddle over the top limb and put the cup over the lower limb.
5. Take the riser of the bow and block the stringer with your foot.
6. Pull the bow up to bend the bow and support the saddle while doing so.
7. When the limbs are sufficiently bent and with the stringer taking the strain, it will be possible for you to slide the string up to the notch on the tip of the limb.
8. Release slowly and remove the bow stringer. Make sure the string is correctly positioned.

If you do not have a bow stringer:

1. Place the smaller loop over the bottom limb in the notches.
2. Place the lower limb of the bow against the ground and hold it in place between your feet. The front of the bow should face to your left.
3. Pull the string up as far it will go. This will be below the tip of the bow. Hold it in your right hand.
4. Bend down so that your shoulder is against the inside curve of the bow
5. With your left hand, pull down on the top of the bow, bending it towards your right hand.

6. Run your right hand up the top limb and curve the bow further.
7. When the bow is sufficiently bent, slip the top loop of the sting into the notches.

It is possible to damage the bow or injure yourself stringing the bow in this way. It is also much more difficult which is why bow stringers were invented.

A compound bow can only be strung with a bow press which you are unlikely to have.

Crossbows: These are essentially a metal or carbon fibre short bow mounted sideways on a wooden stock. Again, there are a number of types. Bolts (arrows for crossbows) are typically wooden with a metal tip or all metal. The bolt lies in a groove and the entire crossbow is aimed. The different types are described below.

Repeating crossbows - These were popular in ancient China. A magazine of bolts sat above the crossbow and the weapon was re-cocked with a hand operated cocking lever. While these had comparatively little power, it was possible to fire around 1 shot per second with an effective range of 60 yards. Clearly, these would not be aimed shots and it is thought likely that they were used in massed volleys. The earliest examples of repeating crossbows have been dated to the 4th century BCE.

Pistol crossbow – This is a small and light crossbow fired with one hand. The draw is typically below 80 lbs and it is cocked ready for fire with a hand operated lever. Modern versions with sights can achieve a fair degree of accuracy when firing from a braced position (a 4-5 inch group at 100 feet) but the bolts are fairly typically fairly light and lose speed rapidly.

Stirrup crossbow – This is a more powerful crossbow that is cocked by putting one foot in a metal stirrup at the front of the crossbow and using the muscles of the leg or back to draw the bow. A typical modern stirrup crossbow has a draw weight of around 165 lbs and fires a typical bolt at around 300 feet per second. These have an effective range of around 300 yards. One shot every 30 seconds would be rapid fire. Typically, these fire a heavier bolt than a pistol crossbow.

Crannequin crossbow – This type uses a small winch to draw back the bow; the winch has to be fitted for reloading and removed for firing. This could have a range in excess of 600 yards but would take several minutes to reload. This type of crossbow would fire a heavy bolt.

While these ranges are impressive, accuracy at those distances is problematic and the reload time makes a crossbow an impractical weapon for use against zombies in almost all circumstances.

Firearms

If you have watched any action movie in the last 20 years, you will have learned a great deal about guns. Unfortunately, these are special Hollywood guns that are rather different from the real thing.

The basics of firearms have not changed a great deal in the last 100 years. A firing pin strikes a percussion cap that contains a small amount of mercury fulminate. This explodes and triggers a secondary explosion in the main cordite charge. This burns very rapidly, propelling the bullet or pellets along the barrel.

Most firearms have a rifled barrel that spins the bullet, greatly increasing the accuracy. Gunpowder is not used in any modern arms and has not been since the late 1800s.

The main areas of variation are in the loading system by which new rounds are loaded, the calibre of the weapon (the diameter of the round) and the length of the barrel. The mechanism for a .22 target pistol and the main gun of a Challenger II tank are otherwise similar.

The only real variation (and this is rarely seen) is the Gyrojet pistol or rifle where the round that is loaded into the chamber contains a small but powerful rocket motor that accelerates and spins the round. They were not very accurate or reliable and were never widely deployed. There have also been a small number of weapons that use electricity to fire the round rather than a firing pin. These have 2 small batteries that power the ignition system. There is no obvious advantage to this approach.

Firearms are not terribly common in the UK and obtaining them post-apocalypse will be difficult but almost certainly necessary for survival. There are, as noted earlier, something like 6 million guns in the UK not counting deactivated and antique guns that can still be fired. Many of these will be in the hands of the military and police forces, specifically Armed Response Units which may be found in larger cities. MOD police are also routinely armed. Shotguns are fairly common on farms and anywhere you see pheasants in the countryside, you will find shotguns close by. There are certainly more than 500,000 shotguns in the UK. Farms are also likely to have rifles or pistols for pest control, typically firing smaller calibre rounds such as .22 long. The highest concentration of guns and the highest number per capita are in Wales, Devon and Cornwall so if you are in the South-West, you will probably have more success while foraging. The area with the smallest legal gun ownership is the city of London. However, illegal guns are remarkably common in cities, generally in homes and lockup garages. This makes it hazardous to search for them given the likely zombie population in the area.

While the military and police do not normally leave guns where civilians can pick them up, they will certainly be bringing out weapons when the zombies start to appear. If the efforts of the military and the police are successful then we don't have an apocalypse to deal with and so this becomes an academic exercise only. However, if they do not manage to control the outbreak (and this is what we will assume as it is the worst case) then they will be overrun and killed or infected.

This means that there will be supplies of firearms and probably small supplies of ammunition in cities from failed attempts to control the outbreak. Whether there is ammunition available will depend on whether they previous owners were overrun because they ran out of ammunition or for other reasons.

Antique weapons are likely to be unreliable for the most part but the definition of "Antique" is very vague and could be considered to include First and Second World War weapons that are still perfectly serviceable. Many older antique guns are flintlocks or matchlocks. These are black powder (gunpowder) guns with the charge and round loaded into the muzzle of the piece. For completeness, here is the technique for loading and firing one of these weapons:

1. With the hammer forward (on a flintlock) or with the match (a burning cord) well out of the way on a matchlock, pour a measure of

powder down the barrel. Most powder horns are designed to deliver a fairly consistent amount of powder.

2. Tamp it down with the ramrod that is normally supplied with the weapon.
3. Put a wad (a cloth or wool patch, possibly fairly thick) into the barrel and tamp it down again.
4. Insert the round.
5. Tamp it down.
6. Insert another wad.
7. Tamp it down.
8. Fill the priming hole with powder. It will normally be necessary to pull back the hammer of a flintlock to do this.
9. If there is a pan for powder (where the hammer/match will go) then fill that with powder also. Some models have a cover that will move out of the way when the hammer moves forward and this protects the powder in the pan. If fitted, use this cover.
10. If not already cocked, cock the hammer or the lever that holds the match (technically referred to as a serpentine).

The weapon is now ready to fire. There will typically be a delay of 1 to 2 seconds between pulling the trigger and the gun firing. Unless the weather is wet or windy, there is about an 85% chance that the weapon will fire when the hammer/serpentine falls. Because the powder loads are not especially consistent and the ammunition is often less than accurately made and the tamping process is not identical each time, accuracy is poor even considering that these are normally smooth bore weapons that do not spin the round. Unfortunately, black powder leaves a considerable residue and it will be necessary to clean the barrel every 5 shots or so. With practice, 3 shots per minute can be fired. I think that you will agree that this is not a practical weapon for use against zombies.

Damage from guns: The amount of energy in a bullet depends on the mass of the bullet and the speed (more technically, the velocity) of the round. The formula is Ek = 0.5 * m * v * v or half the mass multiplied by the square of the velocity. This means that a fast and light round will generally carry more energy than a slower but heavier round. A flintlock pistol had a heavy round with a muzzle velocity of around 1000 feet per second while a modern rifle fires a light round that will typically have a muzzle velocity in the order of 4000 feet per second.

However, the damage is not just based on how much energy is in the bullet since energy transfer is critical. If a round goes through a target without slowing down much (and that is common with soft tissue injuries or grazes) then hardly any of the energy is transferred and so there is very little damage. If the bullet loses all of its energy in the target then the damage is correspondingly great. Various types of round perform very differently in this regard and this will be explained later in this section.

One point to consider is that pistols give a round very much less energy than a rifle – the muzzle energy of a .22 pistol is around 159 joules. A small calibre rifle such as the 5.56 (also .22) standard NATO rifle offers around 1796 joules – more than 10 times the power for the same sized round. How effectively they transmit this energy to the body depends what they hit. Larger rounds typically transfer more energy because they encounter more tissue even though they have less energy due to their lower velocity but they are bulkier and fewer rounds can be carried.

The damage from bullet entry is typically in the form of a rough cone with a small entry point and a large exit wound (if the bullet leaves the body). Contrary to what might be thought, a bullet that leaves the body will typically be less damaging since there is less energy transfer although it will cause more external bleeding. It is useful to contrast this to an arrow or crossbow bolt where the damage is limited to the path of the arrow and bleeding that this causes. High velocity rounds can also cause a phenomena called hydrostatic shock. Human bodies and Sprinters are largely made of water. Shamblers are likely to have a lower percentage of water in their tissues due to leakage from wounds, orifices and general drying. Water is not compressible so a sudden impact is transmitted through body fluids causing damage well away from the original impact site.

In action movies, hits to an arm or leg cause little damage but hits to the body are normally fatal within moments. This is not an accurate portrayal. A high velocity round hitting a limb could do considerable damage due to hydrostatic shock but it is more likely to pass fairly cleanly though soft tissue unless it strikes a bone. A hit to a bone causes significant energy transfer and accordingly considerable damage. When we look at hits to the body, a single shot in the right place will reliably kill but people have survived being shot multiple times in the torso. One man in North Carolina was shot 20 times with a rifle and remained conscious although he was too injured to stand.

The damage done by a bullet falls into two categories; damage that will have long term consequences but which is not immediately disabling and damage that is immediately disabling or fatal. Destroying or significantly damaging the brain will kill anything. Destroying the spinal column will paralyse anything and may kill a human or a Sprinter. A massive loss of blood pressure will quickly render a human or (possibly more slowly) a Sprinter unconscious. It is assumed that Shamblers do not have blood pressure since they are effectively walking corpses.

If we consider PCP users as a fair model for how damage would affect a Sprinter, there are multiple reliable accounts of users running away or driving away after being shot multiple times. Shots that do not cause a massive loss of blood pressure or destruction of the heart, brain or spine are therefore unlikely to rapidly stop a Sprinter. The ability of a round to stop a target has a great deal more to do with where the round hits than it does with the type of round.

Types of gun

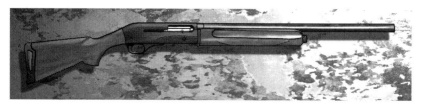

Modern pump action shotgun. Note the slide in front of the trigger that is wracked (a quick forward and back movement) to chamber another round.

Shotguns: These are smooth bore guns and come in single barrel (uncommon), double barrelled (common) and pump action (very rare) types. All types are breech loading – that is to say that the round goes in to the breech rather than down the barrel. With single and double barrelled shotguns, the barrel(s) hinge down and the cartridges are loaded directly into the barrels. With a pump action shotgun, there is a small magazine, normally parallel to the barrel holding around 5 rounds and a sliding handle that moves back and forth to eject the old cartridge and introduce a fresh cartridge. Spent cartridges are removed by hand from the other types. Shotgun shells are normally loaded with shot ranging in size from birdshot (very fine) to buckshot (each ball is about the size of a 30 calibre round). This is designed to spread in flight making the shotgun a very limited area of effect weapon. At short range (less than 5 feet) there will be very little spread and even fine shot will not lose much speed. The multiple balls of shot give very efficient energy transfer and so the damage from a shotgun at short range is formidable. However, the spread means that the damage reduces very markedly with range, especially with fine shot. Having been hit with birdshot fired from 70 yards away, I can report that it stung quite a bit but did not draw blood. Even with buckshot, the effective range of a shotgun is less than 50 yards and damage at this range is unlikely to significantly damage a Sprinter or a Shambler. Double barrelled shotguns have two triggers while other types have a single trigger.

Shotguns often have a spot sight where the user looks down a tube mounted to the top of the weapon. When the brightly coloured line becomes a dot (which will require the correct head position), the dot indicates the aiming point although this will be less accurate at longer range and when firing at different angles. Shotguns may also have simple open sights where the front and back sights are lined up on the target or ring sites where the front site is circular.

Pistols: There are single shot pistols designed for shooting competitions and specialist uses. They typically have a breech loading system similar to shotguns. Most pistols can fire around

6 rounds before needing to be reloaded although there are exceptions such as the Glock 17 discussed earlier in this book. Rounds are stored in a magazine (for a semi-automatic pistol) or in the body of the gun in a revolving cylinder. Modern revolvers are double action. Pulling the trigger rotates the cylinder and pulls back the hammer. With semi-automatic pistols, the recoil is used to re-cock the piece. When loading, it is necessary on the semi-automatic to pull back the slide until it locks. It is possible to load an additional round on a magazine fed weapon by loading a round into the breech and then reloading a single round into the magazine. Doing this increases the tension on the spring and some people believe that this is likely to cause spring failures or jams in the loading mechanism. Pistols generally have a safety switch, typically a slider near the trigger guard although some revolvers do not have such a switch since the heavier trigger pull is considered sufficient to prevent accidental discharge. If you are not actively shooting at a target, the safety catch should be on to prevent accidental discharge of the weapon.

Action movies may have given you some rather odd ideas about how pistols are used. Often you will see them being fired one handed, either with the arm extended but bent or held low near the hip. Sometimes you will see them being fired on their sides. Occasionally, the shooter seems to be trying to flick the bullets out of the gun. While these approaches may be photogenic, they are not recommended if you are trying to hit a specific target. The American police stance is perhaps the best for use against opponents that are not shooting back. The feet are placed a shoulder's width apart and the gun is held in front of the body with the right hand holding the grip and the trigger finger inside the guard. The left hand is wrapped around the right. This gives good stability and the ability to control recoil combined with a clear view of the sights. Given that the target area for a reliable takedown of the zombie is small and ammunition is not going to be plentiful, it is better to spend more time aiming and resist the temptation to fire off several shots in the hope that one will hit and do useful damage. Always squeeze the trigger rather than pulling as any jerky movement will disrupt your aim.

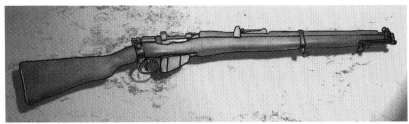

The Lee Enfield Number 4 rifle, Mark 3. This was the main infantry weapon of the Second World War and thousands of this model are still in use as hunting rifles, especially in the US and Canada. This example has the short 5 round clip rather than the longer 10 round clip. The loops under the barrel are for a webbing sling. Modern hunting rifles are very similar although they are likely to be a different calibre.

Rifles, Bolt action: These are breech loading long weapons where the round is inserted and removed by use of a manually operated sliding bolt. There are a number of modern hunting rifles that use a bolt action but perhaps the best known rifle of this type in the UK is the Lee Enfield .303 Rifle 4 Mk 3 (pictured) which was produced in huge numbers over quite a long period including the Second World War with various modifications to the design. There was a (typically) 5 round magazine that was inserted into a receiver in front of the trigger. To operate, the bolt is pushed forward which cocks the action and inserts the round. The bolt is turned to close the breech. After firing, the bolt is turned and pulled back to eject the spent cartridge. Hunting rifles tend to follow the same pattern because it is simple and effective. A rate of aimed fire of one shot every two seconds is possible and a grouping of 4 inches at 200 yards is not exceptional. The accuracy, rate of fire and low ammunition use makes this an ideal type of rifle for use against zombies.

Various types of sight have been fitted to rifles of this type with simple open sights (you line the slot in the rear sight with the vane of the front side), adjustable sights which allow for range adjustment but which can be somewhat delicate and telescopic sights where you line the crosshairs up on the target.

Assault rifles and other modern military weapons used in the UK

The SA80 is the stock British assault rifle. The modified version, the A2, is one of the most reliable and consistent rifles available. The example shown here is the older A1 model with a SUSAT sight. The A2 has a comma shaped cocking handle which is less likely to foul rounds as they are ejected.

SA80: The British military use the SA80, a shorter assault rifle with the magazine behind the trigger that fires NATO standard 5.56mm rounds. This is an advanced rifle with a complex and high precision feeding and firing mechanism. Unfortunately, that means that there is a lot to go wrong and the original weapon is prone to jamming if not kept very clean and well lubricated. Many units were later modified to improve the reliability. The standard magazine is 30 rounds and the effective range is 450 yards with standard open sights, 650 yards with the popular SUSAT sights (an aperture sight with a narrow triangular pillar) and 1000 yards for the long barrel variant. There are a number of variants including one with an under-mounted grenade launcher (40 mm) and the sights fitted can be standard open (or iron) sights, the SUSAT 6 x magnifying sight, a night sight and a laser pointer which can be used in addition to the other sights – obviously this is most useful in low light conditions. Accuracy is excellent for single shots (especially for the longer barrelled variant) and reasonable for automatic fire. There is no burst fire setting. The theoretical rate of fire is 650 rounds per minute. However, the magazine is only 30 rounds and the barrel would melt if you were able to get enough rounds into the rifle to fire for an extended time. To load, place the clip into the receiver carefully (especially if it is the aluminium clip which bends or the plastic clip) with the curve facing the butt and pull back the cocking handle on the right hand side. The safety catch is just above trigger and disengages the trigger from the firing mechanism rather than blocking the trigger.

Fire selector/safety

MP5 machine pistol. There are multiple stock designs but this is a common type. The stock collapses allowing it to be used as a pistol or a carbine length weapon. Note the selector switch used to put the weapon in safe, single shot or (for military variants) fully automatic modes. There is no clip fitted to the MP5 pictured. It fits into the receiver to the front of the trigger guard.

MP5: Used by the British police and certain specialist units of the army, this German made sub-machinegun may be found during foraging. It fires 9mm rounds (there are variants in other calibres but they are not common in the UK) and has a 15 round or 30 round magazine. The most common sight is an aperture type with a single upright pin in the image. Rather than a safety catch, it has a dial selector with 3 positions: S is for safe mode, E is for single shot and F is for automatic fire. There is a cocking lever to the rear of the weapon and this is pulled back and rotated until it locks. The firing mechanism uses an unusually large amount of the weapon's recoil to re-cock the weapon reducing the kick felt by the user. The variant used by the British police does not support fully automatic fire while the versions used by the army do. The British military police use the MP7 which is similar to use but fires the smaller calibre but faster 4.6 mm round giving it superior performance against body armour.

With assault rifles, the bolt may be forward or back when you find the weapon. If it is back then it is likely that there is a round in the chamber. To find out for sure, trap the bolt with your hand (the spring is quite strong) and release it by squeezing the trigger with the weapon pointed towards the ground. When you pull the bolt back again, if there was a round then it will be ejected. Pick it up, wipe off any dirt and keep it because it will be useful.

Sniper rifles: The most common sniper rifle used by the British military is the L115A3 long range rifle. It is more than 4 feet from stock to suppressor with a bipod and a telescopic sight. It is also heavy at nearly 7 KG. It has a 5 round magazine. It fires extremely high velocity 8.59 mm rounds and can reliably hit targets at 500 yards. The longest confirmed kill with one of these rifles is slightly over 2700 yards (2.4 KM). While an incredibly good sniper rifle, it is too specialised to be used in any other role.

Heavy machine gun: These can be vehicle mounted or mobile. If mobile, they will have a tripod. It is belt fed (50 rounds to a belt) and fires .50 calibre rounds which will do very significant damage to any target softer than a tank. It has an effective range of around 2000 yards and can fire up to 635 rounds a minute in theory. In practice, you will run out of ammunition much sooner than that. If you find one, it is likely that there will be additional barrels since high sustained rates of fire will cause significant heating of the barrel and it becomes necessary to swap to a spare to prevent warping.

There are a range of other assault weapons used by the British military and police but they are similar to the weapons described above.

Ammunition

There are multiple types of ammunition with different properties. While you will probably be grateful for any ammunition you can get, it may be helpful to know the advantages and drawbacks of the different types. Most rounds are jacketed lead, the jacket being a thin layer of copper that prevents lead fouling of the barrel. There are exceptions and special purpose rounds that are described below:

Ball: Despite the name, these are typically bullet shaped, a design known as a boat-tail. This type of round is the most common and deforms to a moderate degree on entering the body. It will flatten on hitting a bone, typically shattering the bone at the impact point. It is the type of round most likely to pass through soft tissue with little damage.

Soft point: These are much the same as jacketed ball ammunition except that the front of the bullet is left unjacketed to promote expansion and therefore achieve better energy transfer to the body.

Wad cutter: Originally intended to target work, these flat fronted bullets have excellent energy transfer. They were a common civilian round before the banning of handguns in the UK. They do tend to tumble at range which reduces accuracy but that can improve energy transfer due to an effect known as keyholing. All rounds will tumble if fired through any type of obstacle including vegetation.

Hollow point: These have a hole or dimple in the nose and deform strongly or break up on impact giving superior energy transfer. These are banned from military use by the Hague convention. However, several police forces use these. It is perhaps ironic that we are willing to use weapons on citizens that we are not willing to use on enemies. Because they are designed to deform on impact, they are poor at penetrating any kind of armour. These would be a good choice of round against Sprinters or Shamblers.

Frangible: These are designed to break up into many pieces on impact. The best known brand is the Glazer Safety Slug which have coloured plastic tips. They are exceptionally lethal against unarmoured targets which may make the chosen name seem misleading. Because they expend all of their energy in the body of the target, they do not pass through the target and hit people or objects behind the intended victim making them safer for people not being shot at. They are almost completely ineffective against armoured targets.

Shotgun shells are similar to frangible rounds except that the pellets spread as soon as they are fired. However, it is possible to carefully open shotgun shells and drip melted wax on to the shot to hold it together in flight. Given how inflammable cordite is, the wax should be heated in a pan rather than dripped from a burning candle. Alternatively, there are various types of solid slug of which the Brenneke is the best known. This has fins that cause the round to spin and that reduces friction in the barrel. These offer longer effective ranges and improved accuracy. They are not commonly found in the UK.

Armour piercing: These are typically high velocity rounds that have a core of very hard metal such as tungsten that is designed to pierce metal or other bullet resistant materials. They do not deform much and therefore will not deliver good energy exchange unless they hit bone.

Finally, before leaving the subject of guns, I would like to say a word about automatic fire. In semi-automatic mode, one squeeze of the trigger is one shot. In fully automatic fire mode, it keeps firing while the trigger is held down. So, if you have a 30 round magazine and rate of fire of 10 rounds per second (which the SA80 does) then you have 3 seconds before the clip is empty. When you fire an assault rifle in fully automatic mode, you get a phenomenon known as climb where the muzzle starts to rise. Unless you are braced, the end of the clip is going to be a danger only to birds. Certainly, you will have no accuracy to speak of and your chances of hitting any target more than 10 yards away are slim. The point of fully automatic fire is to allow short bursts and to provide suppressing fire – a hail of bullets that will keep the enemy in cover and not shooting at you.

However, zombies are not going to shoot at you and will not pay any attention to your attempts to intimidate them. Full Auto is not your friend in most circumstances and it is almost certainly a liability when you have limited ammunition. You should keep the selector switch in single shot mode unless "spray and pray" is your only hope. If you have done things correctly, that will never be the case.

Grenades.

These come in a number of varieties, none of which are especially helpful against zombies. Accordingly, the description for each is very brief.

Fragmentation grenades: These are intended for clearing a confined area such as a bunker or a trench. The standard British army grenade is spherical with a spoon shaped lever and a pin. You remove the pin while holding in the lever and throw the grenade. It creates a cloud of fragments that will penetrate all types of personal armour. It is dangerous at a range of 20 metres which is probably considerably further than you can throw it. Variants fired from a grenade launcher can obviously travel further.

Smoke Grenades: These are typically based on white phosphorous and given of large clouds of off-white smoke. The idea of these grenades is to allow unobserved movement and to frustrate enemies who would otherwise fire at troops. However, zombies do not shoot and you will be unable to see any zombies on the other side of the smoke. This is unlikely to be helpful.

"Flash-bangs" or Stun Grenades: These are designed to temporary blind and stun enemies. It seems unlikely that Shamblers can be stunned and Sprinters will be subject to the physical effects only – a large part of the function of these weapons is to mentally shock and frighten the enemy. Given that your team is not likely to be used to these weapons, they are probably something of a liability.

Heavy weapons

The British military have a range of heavy weapons for use against structures and vehicles including the excellent M72 LAW rocket launcher that fires a single use HEAP (High Explosive Armour Piercing) rocket from the shoulder and the Rapier anti-aircraft missile, few of which are much use against zombies. However, there are some lighter weapons that would be effective against the enemies that we will face in a post apocalypse Britain although it may be difficult or impossible to find them.

Mortars: The British heavy military mortar is an 81 mm launching tube that is angled to the required degree; there is a range guide on the base and a sighting mechanism. A mortar round is dropped tail first into the tube. The round will trigger at the base of the tube and launch itself. It normally requires a crew of 3 and weighs just less than 40 KG. It is not practical to carry one of these around. They have a range of 5650 metres or 6180 yards. There is a lighter 51 mm single man mortar (6.2 KG) and 60 mm mortar (22.1 KG). Rounds available for these are high explosive, smoke or flare. The flare rounds remain in the air for longer and burn very brightly illuminating a considerable area. They have a rate of fire of around 15 rounds per minute.

While the high explosive rounds could be handy against a large and closely packed group of zombies, the mortar is both heavy to carry and rather specialised in use. It should also be considered that the mortar shells are neither small nor light. One unique advantage of the mortar is that it is an indirect fire weapon – the bomb goes in a high arc rather than straight at the target. As a result, a mortar can be fired over a wall if needed.

Grenade Machine Gun: This is typically vehicle mounted (it has a lot of recoil) with a 40 mm calibre. It fires high explosive grenades with a nominal rate of fire of 340 rounds per minute. Clearly, this would be a devastating weapon for use against zombies or anything else less armoured than a bunker. If this was a sustainable rate of fire, it would get through nearly 80 KG of ammunition per minute. It has a range of approximately 2 KM. It is very unlikely that you will find one but if you had one of these with a good supply of ammunition, you would be able to handle pretty much any threat.

Improvised weapons

As many revolutions have shown, many things can be turned into weapons with greater or lesser degrees of success. Some require modification, some are dangerous as they are and some can be cobbled together out of commonly available components. However, let us start with a classic.

The chainsaw: A staple of horror movies, the chainsaw is used to lop limbs from zombies and behead them. It is an unstoppable weapon that slices through the undead like a hot knife through butter. However, this is not the movies. The chainsaw is actually quite a poor choice of weapon. To begin with, it is quite heavy at around 7 KG for a low power petrol chainsaw. You are certainly not going to be able to move it quickly or with one hand or for long. The spinning chain makes it especially difficult to handle. Secondly, the saw is not designed for cutting flesh and bone and so will clog on a regular basis which is something of a problem even when using a chainsaw on wood. When a chainsaw hits something denser than it expects, such as bone, then the chain sticks in place for a few seconds. Since the motor is still driving it, the result is that the chainsaw tries briefly to orbit the stuck link. This is called kickback. Since the saw basically becomes uncontrolled at that point, it is very likely to damage the thing closest to it and that will be you. There is a reason that people wear protective clothing while using a chainsaw.

Another point to consider is that chainsaws use quite a lot of fuel and you will need to refill the tank fairly often which means carrying a jerry can of 2 stroke fuel around with you. My experience may not be typical but getting a chainsaw started is not generally quick or easy and may require the precise combination of swear words. Chainsaws are literally deafening which is why users of these tools wear ear defenders. You will be obvious to anything that still has ears and you will not hear them coming. Finally, the action of the chainsaw is such that you will become liberally coated with chewed up zombie flesh, body fluids and bone. Unless you are wearing a space suit, you are almost certainly going to get infected. You will certainly be unable to see or hear. Accordingly, I do not recommend using a chainsaw for zombie destruction.

The Molotov cocktail aka Petrol Bomb: This is a simple weapon. A bottle (ideally thin sided like an old milk bottle) is filled with petrol and rag is stuffed into the top of the bottle. The top of the rag is set alight and the bottle is thrown at something on which it will break, typically a vehicle or the ground near an enemy. These makeshift firebombs are a staple of rioters. As weapons, they leave a lot to be desired. Firstly, the risk of injuring yourself is high. If you have been filling bottles with petrol, you probably have some on your hands or clothes. Holding a burning bottle of petrol is a good way to set yourself on fire. It is possible to drop the bottle or have it knocked out of your hands. Even if you manage to throw it, the range is not great and you are likely to splash yourself or your allies with petrol.

Against zombies, they are of even more limited use. The damage caused by fire is painful rather than immediately incapacitating. It is only our shocked reaction to the pain that stops us when burned. It is unlikely that Sprinters would react the same way although severe burns could compromise their ability to breathe or see. Shamblers would be unlikely to react at all and using a Molotov cocktail on one of those is only useful if you prefer being attacked by a zombie that can burn you in additional to eating you or infecting you.

Explosives: Unfortunately, I am unable to explain how to manufacture explosives because doing so would be against the Explosive Substances Act of 1883. However, the information is available in a number of places should you need it. Manufacturing explosive devices is (at the risk of stating the obvious) extremely hazardous. If you do decide to do so, you should certainly not do so in your main base of operations. Factories designed to make such materials typically have very thick walls and light roofs to channel the blast upwards. I will, however, describe how such devices can be used and the limited utility of them.

High explosives work by burning extremely rapidly with a

release of very hot combustible or non-combustible gases. This causes a shock wave that can stun or seriously injure depending on the size of the explosion and the distance of the target from the centre. This wave of pressure will move along the line of least resistance and do maximum damage where there is no escape route. For this reason, often chimneys are the only surviving part of a house that has been subject to explosive damage – the blast can escape so the chimney is not destroyed.

The initial blast wave can shatter bone and cause cell and organ damage. The blast will generally gather any loose material and this is likely to cause impact and impaling wounds. Dependent on the explosive type, there will be a degree of flash heat that can cause surface burns with damage to the eyes being very common. It is very likely that humans or zombies in the path of a blast wave will be thrown a considerable distance and will suffer additional damage as a result. By packing frangible materials around the explosive device, a considerable amount of shrapnel can be created that will cause lacerations and puncture wounds. The danger of an explosion is very much affected by distance as (ignoring the effect of anything that channels the blast) the force reduces with the square of the distance – objects near the centre of the blast may be disintegrated while objects further away will take much less damage from the initial blast. However, high velocity objects caught up in the explosion can and will travel further and cause damage to anything that they strike. The blast wave is of very short duration but will be followed by rapidly moving air and flame.

High explosives are characterised by a blast that expands more rapidly than the speed of sound. Low order explosives produce a slower explosion. While still very damaging, there is much less of a blast wave as air is able to move away from the explosion.

Debris and other objects will still be thrown a considerable distance and the subsonic pressure wave will still throw zombies or humans away from the centre. The lower order the explosive, the greater the percentage of damage that is caused by heat.

Most explosives that you will have access to are low order explosives. Unless contained in some way (such as in a pipe bomb), these will be less damaging than might be expected. Small high explosive blasts dissipate more rapidly than might be imagined. A concussion grenade is considered lethal at ranges of only around 2 yards. Low order explosives do little to no blast damage although they may stun and cause loss of hearing, burns and carry damaging shrapnel. Someone wearing protective gear that covers the skin will be relatively immune to damage not caused by flying objects or from being thrown away from the explosion.

Given how damaging explosives are, they might seem to be a good weapon against zombies. However, consider that they will be in short supply and dangerous to manufacture. Killing a single zombie would clearly be a poor return on the investment. Indeed, planting explosives in an area that contains zombies is hazardous in and of itself. While an explosive device in a contained area could certainly destroy a lot of zombies in one action, there is unlikely to be an opportunity to get a group of zombies into a room with a large explosive charge. Since the explosion will certainly damage anything in or around the room, it is not a weapon that you would want to use in any area that you have a use for. If you do not have a use for the area, given the risks involved, why would you want to destroy zombies there? You can only reduce or destroy the zombie population in a very limited area and that should be the area that you plan to remain in. Hunting zombies in areas that you do not hold is a waste of resources and dangerous. There will be more zombies drifting in to the area. If you can stay safe and away from the zombies, time will do what a thousand bombs could not.

11. Building a sustainable long term base.

While mobility is the key to staying alive in the early days of the apocalypse, there will come a time when a place that you can defend and survive in becomes necessary. That changes a great deal about the way that you will be working. Rather than taking only what you can carry and avoiding being somewhere where you cannot retreat, having a base means somewhere that is where you go when you retreat. It will be the home for you and your team and so it must be as comfortable and safe as you can make it. Once the immediate needs of survival are handled, morale will become a long term issue and anything that you can do to make life more than bearable will help.

What do I mean when I say that the place must be sustainable? The word is often used as a generic "Green" word in the political sense but, at the core, a sustainable way of doing things means that you can continue to do them. You must have somewhere that will supply at least the bulk of the things that you need. Every time that you need to go foraging, you will risk injury or death to one or more team members so minimising the need to go out to towns and cities that contain zombies or possibly hostile survivors makes good strategic sense. You must make what you have as useful as possible and try to waste nothing.

The place also needs to be safe and there is a great deal that we can do to make an area that we control safe against the threats that we will be facing.

It is obvious that the immediate danger will be zombies but, over time, the threat from zombies will diminish. Sprinters will starve and Shamblers will rot. There may be reinfections but they are probably going to be smaller in number and, by that time, your team should be operating well enough and be sufficiently supplied to handle those. In the short term, this is the threat that you must deal with and I will suggest tactics for doing so.

However, without the people that used to live in the countryside, Britain will no longer be the tame place that we have come to know. Let us look at what, other than humans, live in the UK:

At least 800,000 horses.
10,000,000 cattle
500,000 pigs
36,000,000 sheep
10,500,000 dogs
10,000,000 cats

How much of a threat will they pose? If we assume that they are unaffected by Agent Z then we can draw a fairly accurate picture.

Horses are probably not that dangerous even when wild. Over time, the relatively few stallions will breed and the geldings (castrated males) will die out. They are unlikely to attack us although they could be dangerous if they are panicked. They will eat food crops if they can find them. Stallions may protect their mares against anything that they think could be dangerous. Mares will protect their foals.

Domesticated cows are not especially dangerous, killing only a few people each year. Dairy cows are quite used to people and male cows are castrated making them docile bullocks. However, after a few years, cows will not be used to humans and male cows will be bulls rather than bullocks. They will not have had their horns surgically removed. A fully grown bull can weigh up to 3000 lbs and they are often highly territorial and aggressive, especially the dairy breeds. You will certainly want some way to keep them well away from people. There may, of course be exceptions. There are good natured bulls that have been well treated by humans and these may even seek out human companionship. However, it is better to assume that there is a meaningful risk and be pleasantly surprised in the best case.

If you have lived in the city all your life, you may not have seen pigs except as the filling of a sandwich. However, pigs are not in their natural state pink and in thin slices. Male pigs are castrated when they are young which makes them much less aggressive than they would otherwise. If left uncastrated, domestic pigs are much more like wild boar than the domesticated animal that we know. They are also remarkably intelligent, more so than dogs. While they will not hunt us, they will eat any crops that they can find and they can be dangerous. This might seem like an unlikely claim. However, in an average year, domestic pigs kill around 20,000 people world-wide. There are no figures for injuries but we can reasonably suppose that they are at least 5 times that figure. For comparison, there are around 100 shark attacks worldwide each year and we consider them to be very dangerous. Feral pigs will be a good deal more aggressive than domestic pigs. Pigs typically have litters of 5-6 piglets and will produce one litter every 8 months or so. A single boar and sow can (if there is enough food) produce 60 young over a lifetime. Sows will certainly attack if their piglets are threatened.

Sheep are unlikely to pose much of a threat although rams can be aggressive. Depending on the breed, sheep of either sex may grow horns if they are not removed in infancy so do not assume that any sheep with horns is a ram. Rams can be aggressive while Ewes are only normally a threat when defending their young.

Dogs can very successfully become feral. They will form packs and interbreed. Rather than the huge variety of dogs that we currently have, the mixing of genes will, over several generations, create a robust medium sized dog with no reason to love humans. They may even interbreed with wolves although there are only a handful of these wild cousins of the dog in the UK. These feral dogs will be everywhere and they will be many and, in the winter especially, they will be hungry.

Feral cats may, over time, become large enough to be dangerous but probably not soon enough for it to be a concern to us.

There will also be countless birds, mice, and rats - probably many millions of rats. There are currently thought to be around 60 million rats in the UK. With the increase in the amount of food available to them and the lack of any controls, this is very likely to increase. A female rat can give birth to 35 to 70 offspring each year and rats live for around 3 years if not killed. Analysis performed when estimating the effect of a nuclear exchange suggests that the rat population would explode as large quantities of food (corpses, processed food and crops) became available and then rapidly diminish as those food supplies ended. Animals that prey on rats would probably follow a similar population boom and crash.

If animals are affected by Agent Z, then the picture may be very different. If the pathogen kills them and they do not become zombies then there will be millions of animals rotting in the fields and in hedgerows, in homes and every place. If they become zombies (which is unlikely but a possibility that we must consider) then there will be initially many of these altered creatures and then very few of them as their food supplies dwindle and bacteria destroy them. This land will be a cruel and empty one compared to the once verdant fields and pleasant pastures of memory.

However, there is a predator that I have not listed here and it will be more dangerous than dogs or boar or even the zombies. Walt Kelly, the American writer, identified this enemy nearly 40 years ago: "We have met the enemy and he is us." While many bands of survivors will be happy to set up safe havens and live there, there will always be some people who will want the rewards of success without the hard work. When survival is at stake, there are some who will find that the highest law is the law of the jungle. Your place of safety must be able to withstand these most dangerous of predators. If I am wrong then raiders will not come and you will be safe behind your defences. If they come and you have no defences then all that you have worked for will have been lost. If I am right and you have good defences then you will be safe; we should assume the worst case.

We know what we mean by safe and we know what we mean by sustainable. Unfortunately, anywhere that we choose will be neither of these things in the early days of our stay. We must take a place that has potential and make it what we need it to be. Finding a new home will have to be done without estate agents and glossy photos but at least there will be no mortgage payments.

Where should it be?

The cities will become safer after the number of zombies starts to drop but you can't wait that long before setting up a base. Even if you could, a place in the city will not be easily defensible and there will be no way to grow food once the supplies run out or spoil. A city is a place that can only work with a huge infrastructure to support it and that infrastructure is gone. The city will be a warehouse, a source of knowledge and a place to which humans may return to in the future but it is not a place to live for now.

Small communities have always lived in the countryside and yours can do the same. We can take a lot of our pattern from the pre-industrial world but there is an important difference that we should be aware of. In medieval societies, a town could come under siege from time to time and the procedure was that all food was gathered into a defensible castle or keep and the fields abandoned for the duration of the siege. Sooner or later, the enemy would have to leave and life could get back to normal. However, the besieged would often be starved out and have to surrender. The threats that you are defending against are different. Zombies will not go away until they rot. Wild animals will always be out there. Predatory survivors will not be able to lay siege against you for long but your crops are your most valued possessions rather than gold or political power. You cannot afford to have your productive land outside of your defences. Difficult though it is, you must hold and protect an area large enough to support your community. However, making your new home defensible does not have to be done all at once; there are stages and achievable goals along the way. There must be enough land to support you and that will be a critical factor in choosing your location.

When choosing a place to make a home, you need to consider how many people you currently have as that will determine not only how much space you need but how much space you can hold. You want enough room for everyone and space for a number more. Survivors are likely to join you and babies will be born and grow. You want a base of operations that will serve you well into the future; a sustainable home. If you can't hold as much territory as you want right now, you will need to build expansion into your plans.

For me, the ideal location would be one that has a fair amount of clear ground around it so that there are decent lines of sight, with good drainage, soil suitable for sinking a well and close enough to mature woodland that harvesting trees and firewood will be practical even in winter. I would favour a site on the brow of a gentle hill if possible as that gives a range advantage if you are using bows or guns and makes the site marginally more difficult to attack. That may not be easy if the land does not lend itself to that – East Anglia, for example, is very short on hills. Ideally, I would like to be fairly close to a stream as insurance against the well going dry. Although valleys are more sheltered and flood plains are both flat and fertile, I would sooner be dry when there are very wet years as seems more and more frequent in England in particular. Wales is of course wetter but so much of the country seems to be on a slope that flooding is less of an issue. I will come back to subject of what sort of location that you need for a well later in this section.

The further that you are from a centre of population, the fewer zombies you will have to deal with but the further you will have to go to get anything that has to be salvaged from a town. While the fuel lasts, this is not a serious problem as a 10 mile trip is merely inconvenient. When the fuel has spoiled beyond a usable state, a 10 mile trip carrying supplies is going to be long and difficult. If horses are an option, you will definitely find them a great help but they will have to wait until the threat from zombies has abated.

While you could build a new structure, it is very likely that there is a suitable building in a nearly ideal site, perhaps a farm house or a sizeable country house that would have supported a family and some servants. The people who lived in this region would have known the land and how to use it so they probably made good choices. I would also suggest an older style property as they are easier to defend in the initial stages or if your outer defences are breached; the windows are smaller and any stairs are narrow. Modern buildings often have large areas of glass which may be appealing but that is not easy to make safe against attack. Older style properties are also more likely to have wood burning stoves in the kitchen or in fireplaces – an important point since there will not be fresh supplies of fuel oil or additional gas in the pipes. They are generally less well insulated than modern houses which is a drawback and they may require more maintenance but that is a longer term issue.

Sewerage is, in the long term, likely to be a problem. Older houses may have a septic tank rather than access to sewers. If sewers are available, they is likely to remain functional after Z-day although they may, of course, contain zombies and could be a potential way into your home. It might seem unreasonable to expect sewers to still be working but there is a sewer in Rome that was built in the 5th century BCE and it still serves the city. The risk with a septic tank is that it may contaminate the water table or surrounding land if it is unable to cope with the demands put on it and specialist cleaning companies will certainly not be available. You may need to look at digging latrines, a process described later in this section.

Older buildings may already have a well shaft.

When you have selected a site and a building that should be suitable for a long term base, you will need to make it defensible. It must be possible to defend against a small number of attackers (say twice the number of defenders) with the available team and available weaponry and it must be reasonably resistant to entry when there is no-one defending it. Ideally, it should have a ground floor and an upper floor. If it has a cellar (and few do) then that will be handy for storage of root crops and anything else that is better for being kept a little cooler.

So, your first step will be scouting through the house and ensuring that there are no zombies and no people there. It is possible that such an ideal location already has survivors in it and if so, you may need to negotiate with them to be allowed to stay there. There is strength in numbers and so, if they are reasonable and if you can offer them both food and safety, there is good reason for them to let you join them and make them part of the team. While normally you would want to choose team members based on what they bring to the mix, the person living here brings an ideal location and has survived so far which is the ultimate test of whether they are a survivor or not. Once you are certain that there are no zombies in the house, you will want to make sure that this remains the case.

So, a typical house has a front door, a back door and a number of windows. If it is an old farm house, it is likely that the back door leads into the kitchen and that this will have been designed as a space for a lot of people. Prior to mechanisation, farms took a lot of manual labour. After Z-day and after the fuel spoils, that will become true again. Farm labourers take a lot of feeding and the kitchen may have been used to make food for sale or storage making it larger than might be expected. The back door may well lead to a yard of some sort. Typically, the windows will be smaller than in a modern house but the same principles will apply if it is a more modern building. Additionally, there may be an attached building that also has a door into the house such as a garage or coach-house. All of these will need to be made secure.

Typically, doors in Britain have a type of lock known as a Mortice which has a bolt that slides home when the key is turned and a sprung latch – that is the angled bit of metal that is moved in and out by the handle. These secure one side of the door. Doors typically open in to the house and are secured by 2 hinges. So, when the door is locked, it is anchored at 4 points – the bolt, the latch and the two hinges. Breaking a door down from the outside is much more possible than breaking one down from the inside as the jambs (the bits of wood where the lock and the hinges are) generally block the door from swinging in that direction. The first question that you need to answer for yourself are whether the points of attachment are strong enough to withstand an impact from a running Sprinter – a human will not typically run into a door with as much force as they can muster because they would be injured by the impact. A Sprinter or a Shambler will use as much force as they are able to use. The second question is whether the fabric of the door is strong enough. That will very much depend on the way that the door is constructed.

Internal doors in modern houses are typically light-weight and plain – they are rigid rectangles that appear to be made of wood. In practice, they are mostly made of air. A rectangular frame is built and a thin sheet of wood, often plywood, is put over the frame to make one side of the door. The space inside can be filled with thin wooden slats or increasingly a honeycomb of cardboard to add to the rigidity of the door. A second sheet of plywood is added and you have a light and cheap door. It has very little strength and tapping it and listening will show that it is hollow. This type of door is clearly not strong enough. Alternatively, the space inside the door can be filled with low density fibreboard or foam which is stronger and offers better insulation but is still much less robust than a solid door. There are panel doors which are frames with cross pieces and (obviously) wooden panels although some hollow doors have plastic mouldings that make them look like panel doors. UPVC doors are typically reasonably strong and some have metal frames. Wood doors can also have a metal core designed to make them more resistant. These are typically heavier with longer hinges and multiple bolts along the frame. Doors such as these will be suitable for withstanding attack without being replaced although any glass will need to be covered with wood planking, metal sheet or metal strips.

Although an older type of door, ledge or ledge and brace doors may be found in traditional houses. These are vertical planks (often joined with tongue and groove) held together with horizontal ledges (additional planks) or with ledges and a diagonal brace. Braces can be added to ledge doors as can additional ledges. These are fairly robust although age may have softened the wood. Stable type doors are typically ledge and brace doors that open in two sections. These can be joined with the addition of planks although they will still be weaker than would be ideal. Metal sheet can be added to any door to make it more resistant, ideally to both sides of the door with multiple attachment points such as bolts driven through the door. Hollow core doors are not really strong enough and should be replaced if possible. If this is not possible then you will need to toughen them with metal plates as best possible but the frames are still likely to be weak.

If the door is sufficiently strong then increasing the number of points where it attaches to the frame is possible. Hinges can be added as can additional bolts. Doors from an adjacent structure such as a garage may be internal doors and so weaker than needed and if there is a cellar then it will often have a coal chute or other access route that is protected only be a metal flap. If so then you will want to address this. At the very least, you will want to add a padlock.

Windows are harder to fortify because glass is an intrinsically fragile material. Metal or wooden bars can be added as can shutters, either metal or wood and locking with a hasp and padlock. While zombies are unlikely to open shutters, human attackers can and zombies may be able to rip the shutters off unless they are very sturdily attached. The safest option is to brick up ground floor windows with only a small slit or a couple of small slits to provide light and air. Windows above the ground floor will need less protection although human attackers are able to climb. Bars can be fitted to these but that will make it more difficult for defenders to attack people on the ground.

There will be times when you will have fewer or possibly no people in the base – typically during foraging expeditions. One possibility that needs to be considered is that someone or something has entered the house while you were away. While making the doors as secure as possible is certainly helpful, it is very useful to have warning that this has happened and for this I recommend what I refer to as flags. A flag is a clearly visible strip of something (packing straps are ideal for this purpose) that you leave tucked into the door frame when you leave; ideally they should always be in the same position so that it will be clear if someone has moved them. When the door is opened, the strip falls down. If you return and the flags are not in the frame or look to have been moved then it is likely that there is someone inside the house. You do not want to walk into an ambush. Treat entering the building in the same way as you would when entering any other unknown space.

Once the building is reasonably secure, you have a base of operations, a place to live and plan. Of course, there will be issues that you will need to confront. The first is that there is no electrical power – or if there is, it is from a backup generator. Having this is a great advantage but it will be difficult to keep it fuelled especially as the fuel starts to deteriorate. If there is heating, it is probably oil fired and that will work until the oil runs out... if it will run without electricity which some heaters will not. If you find that you have oil heating and a generator then you are in a fortunate position as this gives you time to plan on how to live without these things. To make the house sustainable, it will have to run off things that can be found or made locally. With an older property, it will have been designed with that in mind and there will be chimneys and fireplaces that can be brought back into service. If you are lucky, there may be a wood burning stove as these are very effective at making a place habitable.

Wood fires (and to a greater extent, coal fires) cause a build-up of soot and oil in the chimney. When this layer gets thick enough, it can catch on fire. This fire tends to be very hot, sometimes over 1600 degrees C. This is hot enough to melt iron. If there is thatch, it will almost certainly burn. Bricks are likely to be seriously damaged. It is possible that the fire will spread. For this reason, it is necessary to sweep the chimney from time to time when build-ups of this material are noticed. It is also possible for chimneys to be blocked by bird nests. These should be cleared and birds discouraged from nesting.

Water is more of a problem. Before Z-day, we all use a great deal of water, on average about 150 litres a day. Most of this is used in washing, flush toilets and so on. Very little of this is drunk. Most buckets are around 15 litres so that is 10 brimming buckets per person per day. If you have a 5 person team, that is 750 KG of water, a full three quarters of a ton of water to move every single day. When it does not come out of pipes, that is going to be difficult. The water that we use comes mainly from reservoirs and aquifers and it processed (filtered and chlorinated) and stored in distribution reservoirs. It is pumped into the pipes from there. These pumps are powered from the national grid but they have back-up generators to allow them to run for a time after a power failure. In the case of a breakdown of society, water supplies will outlast the national grid but not by more than a day or so.

When you consider that you will be growing crops as well which will need water for at least some of the year, you could be looking at well over a metric ton of water per day. Saving rainwater will help but not be enough to meet your needs. You are going to need a well.

The classic design for a well is a long shaft into the ground with a brick or stone liner that extends a few feet into the air with a small roof and a winch mechanism for pulling the bucket up and down. The good things about this design are twofold. The first is that it works. The second is that it requires very little technology to create.

You will need:

Spades
A pick axe

Buckets
Rope
A pump
Measuring tape or at least a marked off length of string
Brick or stones or well rings for lining the well. Well rings can be cast if needed but they should be available with a little foraging
Strong backs

Here is how to build one:

1. Ideally start in the summer because you will need to reach the aquifer as it will be in the driest season. Because this is Britain, summers could be very dry or very wet so there is a degree of chance in this that we cannot eliminate.
2. The best place for a well is actually on a rise in the land. The water table (which is what you need to reach) follows the surface of the land to a degree but you need to reach down to an aquifer which is significantly below the level of the water table. The water table is the level at which the soil is wet enough that a hole will fill with water. This water will be loaded with organic materials and soil bacteria including anthrax. You will need to reach down into the deeper levels to obtain clean ground water. If you have to dig latrines in addition to a well, these should be at the opposite end of the territory that you control to minimise the risk of contamination. Of course, there needs to be an aquifer to dig down into – ultimately, there will be bed rock under all soil although it is much closer to the surface in some places than others. While it is possible to know for sure with techniques such as ground penetrating radar, these are unlikely to be available to you. However, a useful clue is the presence of deep rooted trees that

remain green and lush in the height of summer. Aquifers are bodies of water within porous stone – chalk, limestone, sandstone and greensand are good types of rock for this. Other rocks may have smaller quantities of water but places with igneous rocks such as basalt and granite are likely to offer little water and so these are poor areas for a well. Typically, wells will need to go down for at least 3 metres in the UK and may need to be as deep as 18 metres. The deepest known hand dug wells go as far as 60 metres down. If you have to go deeper than 18 metres, you are in a poor area for a well. Much of Cornwall, Wales, Scotland and some parts of Ireland have rock types that are less permeable and therefore difficult. Anywhere where there are chalk downs or limestone or sandstone is likely to be suitable although you may have to dig a long way.

3. To start, decide how large the well must be. Typically this needs to be large enough for two people digging. Start digging a circular hole. In the early stages, it is easy (relatively speaking) to put the earth by the side of the hole. Later, it will be necessary to raise the earth with a bucket or box on a rope. The process is very labour intensive.

4. You will need to line the well as you dig down. This used to be done with stone or brick but cast well rings are a better option. You will have seen these on building sites and beside roads without necessarily knowing what they are. They are short cylinders of concrete, typically about 3-4 feet across. They normally interlock with other rings of the same type. You will need a foraging trip to get these. They are heavy and something like a flatbed truck will be needed to move them effectively. You will need to take into account the size of available well rings when choosing a diameter for the well.

Smaller rings need less digging but give less room for the digger or diggers. You will certainly need these to line the well in the parts that are within the soil layer but if you are digging through solid rock, this should prove tough enough as long as it is not significantly fractured. If the rock remains loose, you will need well rings all the way down. Foot holes can be cut in the rings with a chisel. It will sometimes be necessary after construction to go down the well to clean it.

5. As you dig down, water will start to fill the hole and this will need to be pumped out before you can continue to dig. The more clean water that you have to pump out, the closer that you are to having a working well. The well liners in the soil should mean that little of the water is surface water. You can further minimise this by sealing the well rings in the upper section with cement.

When you are having trouble pumping out enough water to dig further down and the water is clean, you have a well. At this point, add an additional well ring or bricks at the top to prevent anyone or anything falling down the well and put a lid on it.

Before constructing a well of this type, search the grounds carefully for an existing well. Typically these were not filled in but just capped with wood or stone. It is probably going to be a lot easier to repair an old well than it would be to dig a fresh one. There may be grass covering a cap stone so pushing an iron rod into the ground can be a useful approach.

Well water should still be boiled before drinking or using it to clean injuries. It is probably sufficiently clean for washing without further treatment.

If you have access to a pump and you are confident that you

will continue to have access to it, it is possible to drive a much narrower hole with an auger and pump water from the bottom of that. However, there is a problem with any type of suction pump. These work by reducing the pressure above the water; the water is pushed up into the pipe by atmospheric pressure. A column of water 33.9 feet high will exert a downward pressure of 1 atmosphere and so balance out any pump no matter how strong. A bucket on a rope does not have this limitation. If it were possible to put the pump at the bottom and push the water up then the limiting factor would be the strength of the pump.

Latrines

While it is likely that the building that you have occupied will have flush toilets, it is possible that the number of people that you have will exceed the capacity of those toilets and water will need to be brought to flush the toilet after it is used. In that case, it will be necessary to dig latrines. There are multiple types of these ranging from a makeshift arrangement just off the road while travelling to a semi-permanent solution of the type that I will be describing. These are based on military camp guidelines.

To build a latrine:

1. The first thing to decide is the placement of the latrine. It should be well away from your water source (at least 100 feet with further being better) and away from the house. Ideally, it should be downslope from the house if the land is not level.
2. Dig a slit trench. In practice is difficult to dig a deep slit

so you may need to dig it wider than would otherwise be necessary. How long a latrine will continue to work for depends on the level of use and the depth. Since the contents will rot down, a deep enough pit with light use will last a considerable time. If the rate at which it fills is high, you will have to move the latrine more often or dig the latrine out more often. Neither of these are pleasant jobs. It will probably be necessary to line the pit with planks to prevent it from collapsing. A depth of around 6 feet is necessary. If it is possible to make it deeper, it is a good idea to do so as this will reduce the smell. If the water table is near the surface then you will need to build a mound latrine which is exactly what it sounds like – a mound with a latrine built on top.

3. Build a box and bench arrangement. You will need to construct a frame for supporting seats with a suitable hole in them for solid and liquid waste. Roman toilets used a slab of wood or stone with keyhole shapes cut out. While the Romans did not bother with dividing walls, your team may be more comfortable with some form of divider. A simple structure would be a rectangular frame with 2 or more divisions braced with 2 crosspieces with small gap suitable for a divider and supporting legs. The divider can be planks or wood sheets depending on what is available. The seats will be made of cut planking. Care should be taken to avoid splinters for the obvious reason. A similarly sized frame can be used to form the roof – the legs of the lower frame can continue up to head height. Sides, a back and doors are added to this frame to make a single movable unit. Add bracing as necessary to make this reasonably rigid. If there are strong winds in the region, you will want to anchor this with guy ropes or weight it with waste material such as old car tires. If you decide to

weight it, you will need to build it more sturdily. However, it has to be built so that it is movable.

4. The latrine is used in the usual way. A pail of ashes or chopped straw should be provided to cover waste as this will reduce the unpleasant smell and discourage flies.

5. Periodically, it will be necessary to perform an operation known as peak knocking. The nature of solid waste is that it tends to form mounds. With a suitable pole, these mounds will need to be evened out. The smell while performing this operation is, to say the least, remarkable. This is much easier to do if the frame is moved first.

6. If the pit is filling up, it can be dug out with spades and the rotted down waste put into wheelbarrows. If tubs with perforated lids are available, it can be left to rot down for a season and then mixed with compost. The high nitrogen levels are very helpful to plants. Alternatively, a new latrine can be dug.

Urine can be added to a compost heap directly. The nitrogen and phosphorus in urine are essential plant nutrients and the urine breaks down plant material to a degree. Anyone with a shy bladder can use a bucket to deliver these if preferred.

Planting trees that use the nutrition in waste will reduce the amount of emptying that needs to be done. Willows are especially suitable for this purpose and will help to give at least an illusion of privacy.

Re-using waste for compost heaps is an example of how to make a settlement sustainable. If something can be used then it should be used because this will reduce the number of trips outside the compound you need to make. Each time you leave, there is a risk that you will not make it back. All plant, human and animal waste can and should go back into making the soil richer.

Securing the compound

Man has enclosed his settlements for as long as he has been a tool user. Iron Age villages used an enclosure that looked like an Omega sign from above. The Romans favoured a rectangle with rounded corners. Medieval enclosures were irregular shapes based on land boundaries. Traditionally, ditches or log stockades were favoured but there are other options:

Barbed wire: This was used extensively to interdict areas in the First World War with stakes used to peg the wire in place. It entangled soldiers and held them in place long enough to be shot. It would be reasonably effective against zombies. However, if there are many zombies, the first few to be caught in the wire will effectively act as bridges. Humans can cut the wires or approach in a vehicle. While this is likely to be damaged by the wire, it won't do enough damage to stop it. This could be used as a temporary defence while a stockade or wall was created.

Ditches: Ditches were often used to mark boundaries and are useful to prevent cattle and sheep straying. They have also been used defensively with the Roman army having a standard set of rules for building a steep sided ditch that was difficult to climb out of. The soil dug from the ditch would be piled on the side of the ditch closest to the compound. While this would need to be defended, it would be a major tactical advantage in a conflict. A palisade could then be built on the raised ground inside the ring ditch. This allows a two stage build without wasted effort. A large enough ditch will also stop vehicles.

Stone walls: The staple of the medieval period, stone walls are robust, secure and very durable. They can be climbed but not by zombies and they are easily defensible. However, consider the amount of stone that is needed. The volume of the wall is the length x width x height and you must allow for the footing of the wall. Let us say that this is 25% more stone. A 200 metre long wall that was 0.3 of a metre thick and 2.5 metres high is 150 cubic metres of stone which comes to about 490 metric tons of rock. You probably want a longer wall than this and you cannot patrol such a narrow wall. If you make it a meter wide then you have 1462 tons of rock. That is probably several man-years of work. It might be possible in the very long term but you are going to need something faster in the meantime.

Palisades: These are tree trunks sunk vertically into the earth and sharpened at the top. They are difficult to climb even for a human and will stop a vehicle. They will eventually rot but sections can be replaced one at a time. They have been the preferred choice for hasty fortifications from the Stone Age. That is what I would recommend.

To build a palisade:

1. Dig a trench. You will want between 25% and 33% of the log underground. The profile of the trench should be flat toward the side that you are defending from, flat at the bottom and sloping outwards slightly towards your base. That is so that when you place the logs, you can slide them down and then butt them squarely.
2. If you can, pour some concrete into the trench to provide a base. If you cannot, stones will do. Wood

placed directly onto the soil will rot faster. If neither concrete nor stones are available, soil will have to do.

3. Take a palisade section (described below) and place it next to any existing section of palisade wall with the blunt end next to the trench.
4. Slide it forwards so that it stands in the trench. The angle will help to keep this controlled. The section will be tilted initially and you will need to get it upright by pushing and pulling. Wedge it in place with stones or pour concrete if available.
5. Join the new section to the existing section with 2 or 3 horizontal bars, the lowest of which should not touch the ground.
6. Pack earth into any gaps where the log has been planted.
7. Repeat as needed.

To build a section, you will need some thick logs and some thinner beams or bars. You will want logs of about the same thickness and at least the height of the wall plus 33%. Pine forests are ideal as a source for trees that are suitable for this use since they tend to have been planted at the same time and so are about the same width and height. Sharpen one end of each log to a point. Lay them next to each other and place a bar across the length of the section at just over 1/3 of the distance from the bottom (so it will be a little way above the ground), another just before the sharpened section and a third in the middle. Using long nails or bolts, secure the bars to the logs. If long bolts are not available, the bars can be lashed in place with rope but this is not as strong. You may have to do this with curved sections or use multiple shorter bars.

Obviously, this is a lot easier if you can find a mini-digger and a chainsaw. Both of these items should be possible to find in the countryside relatively easily as many farms have them. Chainsaws are also available from many larger DIY stores and from tree surgeons who typically advertise in local papers. While they are no longer going to be open for business, this will tell you where to look for equipment. I recommend picking up any protective gear that you find. The previous owners bought it for a reason. Local papers and directories are worth collecting if you find any since they will give additional information about tradesmen (and therefore caches of tools) in the area.

Because there are probably very limited or no defences for the area that you are enclosing, you will want some of your team putting up the palisade and some of them guarding with whatever weapons are available. You will probably want to alternate the teams as this is heavy manual work.

There are likely to be small gaps between the logs and you have two options. You can fill the gaps with a mixture of mud, straw and (if available) cow dung or you can leave the gaps as firing loops for guns, bows or spears since that will allow you to attack an enemy while still in excellent cover.

As a rule of thumb, following ancient Roman patterns is a good idea. They were experts at creating a low technology but high utility infrastructure.

It is possible to build more mobile temporary barriers called Cheval de Frise. The term (which means "Frisian horse") refers to a multiply spiked barrier. To make one, you will need a long straight log that has holes cut or drilled through it at right angles, alternating up and down the length of the log with wooden spikes or sharpened branches running through them.

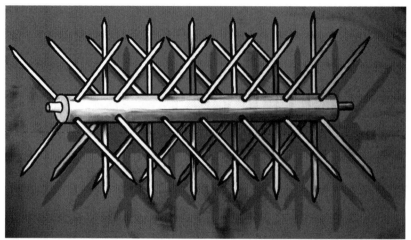

This Cheval De Frise has a central spike which stops horses from jumping over it. You can omit this if you wish but remember that you will also want to defend against humans.

These barriers can be used to protect the area around the work crew and will be useful later for additional defences around the gate. The gate will simply be a hinged section of palisade. However, I recommend building a double gate where the outer gate leads into a box made of palisade. The purpose of this is threefold. The first is that the gate is always a weak spot and so having an additional line of defence is an advantage. The second is that this is a good area to check that no-one who has been on a foraging trip is infected and to wash down the vehicles before they enter the compound proper. The third is that you can allow a small number of people into the box to allow them to talk with you without letting them into the compound and without them being at risk from the environment. It may be that they are a group from another settlement looking for help or trade but it does no harm to be safe.

All of these improvements require wood to create and so you

will need to be able to find a source. There are lumber yards and pre-cut timber in builders merchants all across the country but you want to minimise the number of foraging trips so anything that you can produce locally should be produced locally. If you have a chainsaw, felling trees is not especially difficult. I would urge you to wear any protective clothing designed to stop a chainsaw blade. It is all too easy to slice into a leg or cut off a finger.

To fell a tree, you need to find one of the right size that has somewhere clear to fall. It may be necessary to trim off some branches if the tree is in dense forest but it normally possible to take one from the edge of managed woodland. You need to make a V-shaped horizontal cut into the tree removing a wedge to roughly half the thickness of the tree. It will fall in that direction if it is on level ground. You should take any lean in the tree into account when choosing where it should land. Once you have cut the wedge, you cut from the other side of the trunk to the point of the V with the chainsaw and the tree will fall. Obviously, care should be taken to ensure that it does not fall on any structures or people. Once the tree is down, the larger limbs can be removed with the chainsaw making it easier to drag. These branches are useful for firewood or for making smaller wooden items and should not be wasted. The trimmed log is probably too heavy to carry back even with multiple people – a 20 foot long log that is 10 inches in diameter weighs around 400 lbs or 180 KG. However, it can be dragged back and if you have one or more quad bikes or tractors, this will be much easier.

Because the palisade blocks your view of the outside world, you will want to add a watch tower, especially if your building is single storey or if the land is on a slope. The watch tower should be at the highest point. The easiest way of constructing one of these is to dig 4 post holes suitable for holding a thinner tree trunk in a square pattern with a hole at each corner. The depth should be around a quarter of the length of the posts since there will be less stress on these posts than there would be on the palisade walls. You can add a floor at the appropriate height by cutting notches into the beam and inserting sturdy planks that will support a larger floor. The logs above a point where a tall man's head would be if he were standing on the floor can be cut off at an angle to support a sloping board roof. Planks should be added to the outside to provide a degree of shelter and to prevent the watch person from falling.

With a decent palisade, upstairs windows and even homemade ranged weapons, you have a safe place to live and those, after Z-day, will be rare indeed. Well done.

There is one thing left to do to complete your protection and that is to set up a quarantine room, ideally more than one. It should not be possible to open the door from the inside and you are going to want a flap in the door large enough for a tray of food and a slop bucket. It will be necessary for everyone to understand that going into the quarantine room is not a punishment; it is a way of protecting everyone and sooner or later, everyone will probably spend some time in there. Anyone who has any kind of disease that could be infectious is going to have to go in there for the good of the larger group. If you have multiple people who could be infectious, you are going to want to separate them from each other as much as from everyone else. If someone does have Agent Z, there is probably only one treatment that you can apply. The body will need to be disposed of well outside of the compound and you will need to wash down everything with a strong bleach solution. Any fabrics and anything that cannot be sterilised in any other way will need to be burned.

Food and farming

You will want to make every scrap of land work for you, not just the first season but every season. That will mean growing the right crops and doing what you can to keep the soil in top condition. The question of what you raise will inevitably be a compromise between what you need, what is available and what can survive on the land that you have.

It is possible, as discussed, that animals will be in short supply because they were affected in some way by Agent Z or they have been killed by zombies. However, they may be plentiful. If so, should you include livestock in your farming? There is no doubt that meat is tasty and protein is important in a diet. However, there are some factors that you need to consider before you decide to raise livestock:

1. Meat production is not efficient. Pigs will put on 1 KG of weight for every 2.5 KG of food that they consume. Cattle need nearly 6 KG for a 1 KG gain. Sheep need at least 1 KG of high energy sheep pellets food just to maintain weight and nearly twice that to gain any weight. If you have a limited food supply (and you will) then feeding it to animals will reduce the total amount of food available.
2. Animals will need space to live and that is land that you cannot grow other crops on. Even if you keep the animals in the most confined space possible, that is a double hit on your food supply.
3. Most new variants of viruses occur when a virus moves between species and this has been the source of the

great influenza epidemics. With proper control, this can be avoided but it is a risk to consider. This always happens when animals and humans live in close proximity.

If you find yourself craving meat, the forests will (unless they have been affected by Agent Z) be full of game after a few years. If you do decide to raise livestock, pigs will probably give you the most meat for the amount of feed given to the animal. Chickens are also a good option as they give both eggs and meat. Fat from animals can be stored for long periods in airtight containers.

We have grown used to all foods being available in supermarkets all year round. This is a luxury that you will no longer have. The biblical quote applies: "To every thing there is a season and a time for every purpose". You will have to grow what you can when you can.

Spring:

Beans (late spring) and peas (early to middle spring) will be a staple of harvests early in the year. Before potatoes were introduced into the UK, peas and beans were a much larger proportion of the diet of the average Briton. They are nutritious and they can be dried for storage. In terms of yield, they are a good choice. They can be sown from February if the weather is mild. They will need canes or lattices to climb up. Bean and pea sprouts are both tasty and nutritious. The stalks and leaves of older plants are not especially edible (they become woody) but will improve the quality of compost. Beans will tend to increase the nitrogen in soils which other plants put into the same area in subsequent seasons will need. Red coloured beans typically need to be cooked to destroy toxic chemicals in the bean.

Soybeans are not a reliable crop in the UK as they need a long hot summer, a rarity in this country.

Spring greens and brassicas such as cabbage, broccoli and Kale all have spring cropping varieties and are typically sown in late autumn. It should be noted that brassicas tend to require soils rich in minerals and prefer lighter soils. Crops can be taken from brassicas such as Brussel sprouts for a number of months. Kale can also be harvested without killing the plant and contains surprising amounts of iron, calcium and magnesium. Cabbages are harvested as a complete head but a new head will grow if the stem is left. If cut in a cross pattern, 4 smaller heads will typically grow. Of course, not everyone likes brassicas, especially Brussel sprouts, and the sugars in them can cause flatulence. However, it is food and hunger is the best sauce. All of these vegetables can be pickled to preserve them.

Since these plants are in the ground in the winter, it is a good idea to protect them from frost. Old clothing, plastic sheeting and glass cloches (little sheet glass tents over the plants) can help considerably.

Spring onions are quick growing and can be sown in spring for harvest in a number of weeks.

Summer:

Broad beans, runner beans, some varieties of cabbage, carrots, pumpkins, radishes, lettuce, peppers, onions, sweetcorn and tomatoes are all vegetables that crop throughout the summer. Beans can obviously be dried as can sweetcorn. Carrots and onions can be stored through the autumn and into the winter. Cabbages can be stored for weeks or months in a cool cellar. They should be stored on a tray not touching each other in cool moist air. Mature carrots can be kept in similar conditions for up to 6 months although damaged carrots should be eaten at once as they store poorly. Pumpkins and other squashes can be stored for up to 6 months but require drier conditions with good ventilation, as cool as possible without risking frost. Again, they should be stored on wooden boards and not touching each other. Onions require similar conditions. The other crops do not store well although most of these pickle well, especially onions.

Autumn:

Many summer crops will continue into the autumn. Crops that will typically only be ready in autumn include Parsnips, Swede (which will continue into the winter), Leeks (which will continue until early winter), Beetroot, Garlic, Cauliflower and Aubergines. Fruit trees such as Apple, Pear, Plums, Gooseberries, Blackberries and cherries will all be ready for harvest in autumn. Some will last into the winter with Swede and Parsnips storing well in the soil as long as it is not too wet. The fruits can be bottled or made into jam if sugar is available. Cauliflower will store reasonably well in cool conditions and can be pickled. Apples can be stored in dry conditions, separated from each other.

Potatoes can be early crop (spring) or maincrop (late autumn) and store well in cool, dark and dry conditions. While not a flavour explosion, they are always welcome and provide (perhaps surprisingly) a good supply of protein in addition to the obvious carbohydrates.

Winter:

Few things grow well in winter but there are options. Rhubarb is a good source of vitamin C and can be persuaded to grow throughout the winter if it protected from frost by putting a collar around the plant. It will grow up to the sunlight. The stalks are edible but have a very tart flavour. The leaves contain dangerous levels of oxalic acid and should not be eaten. Most winter crops will continue only until early in the winter with the milder weather in the south of the country extending the season. For this reason, you will want to store as much of the autumn production as possible. Stored vegetables and fruits should be inspected every few days for spoilage. Any that show signs of rot should be removed before the decay can spread to other fruit or vegetables.

The leaves and shoots of potatoes and tomatoes are poisonous (the plants are related) due to the high levels of Oxalic acid. However, most food crops can be used almost entirely. Turnip greens are well known although they have a somewhat bitter flavour. Turnips, sprouts, cabbages and other brassicas all have edible greens. While they do contain traces of cyanide, this is not dangerous although it does causes some people (dependent on genes) to perceive them as very bitter. Sauces can make any meal more palatable.

You can also forage for supplies in the winter and this will be necessary if you have not managed to store enough food to last until the spring. Fortunately, Sprinters are likely to suffer from exposure and Shamblers are likely to move very slowly in the colder weather making them less of a threat.

Because plants are affected considerably by climate and soil conditions, it is likely that the best growing seasons and the best varieties for your region will be different from those in other parts of the country. The best advice that I can offer is to see what others have found grows well. For example, if the fields that you pass are full of maize, that is probably a good crop for the area. If you have a heavy clay soil then carrots (for example) are unlikely to grow well. It is possible to create raised beds with a layer of soil different from the natural soil but you will probably get better results from raising plants that suit the local conditions.

You will want to change which plots are used to grow each type of plant as that will give the soil time to recover and reduce the risk of diseases lingering in the earth. Compost should be dug into the soil to improve its texture and add nutrients.

When foraging for seed, it is important to be aware that many vegetables are F1 Hybrid varieties. While these tend to offer good disease resistance and yields, they are produced by crossing different strains of the plant. The seeds of these vegetables will not breed true; they will revert to the characteristics of their parents or different mixes of the parental plants. A number are incapable of producing any fertile seed for a second generation. Older varieties are less vigorous but will produce fertile seed.

If you have a base close to the sea or to a river, you can catch fish to supplement your diet. Angling with a fishing rod will be your best option if you live on the coast although there is no guarantee that you will catch anything. Angling gear is available in most seaside towns with a little searching. Bait is normally available by digging in mudflats although care should be taken not to become trapped in the mud. The worms found there will be quite acceptable to a range of fish.

In rivers, fish traps are an option. These are constructed of wicker or wire and are thin cylinders closed at one end, generally coming to a point. A fish that swims into one of these cannot turn around and so is trapped. They can be set and checked daily for fish. Care is needed as this does expose you to a degree of risk from being outside the safety of the compound. Inland, it is possible to create fish ponds and this was a popular option during the medieval period. These ponds require minimal maintenance and the fish will feed themselves.

To create a fish pond, you will need an area suitable for a large pool of standing water or a stream suitable for damming. If you do not have a constant stream of fresh water, it will be necessary to plant wetland plants to keep the water fresh. These can be found in streams and should be lifted carefully so that the roots are intact and transported in water. Even if there is a fresh water supply, these will encourage fish and so are worth planting. If the soil drains freely, it will be necessary to put a water-resistant layer of materials down. You will be able to find large sheets that can be overlapped in builder's merchants or clay, concrete or sand can be used. Dig out an area suitable for the pool and waterproof it as needed, whether it is a free standing pool or an extension to an existing stream. Allow the area to fill with water. It will not be practical to fill a pool of this size from a well but a stream will provide the required water if available. UK rainfall will generally fill a well sealed pool and the transplanted plants will keep the water from becoming stagnant. Obviously, the plants will need a certain amount of soil and gravel to root in and spread. The ecosystem of the pond will need some time to develop before you can stock it with fish. Since the time required will depend on the conditions, it is better to judge the condition of the pond by what is living there. You will want to see insects and a spread of water plants before it can be considered suitable for fish. When it is ready, stock the pond (if necessary) with suitable freshwater species. These are easiest to obtain from a nearby lake and they will be suitable for the local climate. Predatory fish such as pike will need a large number of smaller fish to act as food.

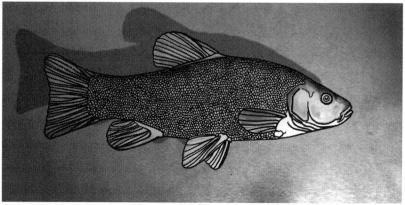

An adult Tench. These fish are brown to green in colour and often exceed a foot in length and can weigh up to 2 KG. Maggots and worms are good bait for catching this species since worms are their natural diet. They have a muddy flavour not dissimilar to Trout.

Tench are a very suitable species for this type of pond and will not feed on smaller fish. If the pond is fed by a stream, fish are likely to move into the area. You should ensure when stocking the pond that you have both male and female fish. After a few generations of fish, the population should be stable enough to harvest a small number of fish throughout the year.

If a fish pond freezes, the amount of oxygen in the water will drop rapidly and the fish will die. Accordingly, you will need to break any significant ice cover that forms in the winter.

Another possible source of food is hunting. The main types of game available in the British countryside are deer and game birds, most commonly pheasants that were bred for hunting. There is also small game such as rabbits and hares. You will almost certainly need to conserve your ammunition for use against zombies but animals can be hunted successfully with bows or trapped with snares. Snares are an illegal form of trapping prior to Z-day.

To make a snare

1. Cut a piece of wire about 20 inches long.

2. Bend the wire into a small loop about 1.5 inches from one end. Using pliers, twist the wire until the loop is formed. If the loop comes loose then the rabbit can escape so ensure that the wire is well joined.

3. Bring the other end of the wire through the loop. This will form a larger loop that will capture the rabbit around the neck.

4. Form another small loop on the end of the wire you just brought through the first loop, twisting it as before. This loop should be about 1.5 inches across.

5. Attach a length of string to the second loop that you have just formed. The other end of this string will need to be tied around a sapling or bush to draw the snare tight when the rabbit tries to run forward.

Snares should be checked daily. Rabbits are most commonly active at twilight and at night. When you find a rabbit, check that it appears healthy before preparing it for eating as myxomatosis is common in British rabbits. While it cannot infect humans, it is inadvisable to eat the meat of ill animals. As a side note, myxamatosis was introduced into the UK deliberately and killed 90% of the rabbit population. If you are reading this section after Z-day, you may find it ironic that humans used a biological weapon on another species so successfully.

Pheasants are active in the daytime and will, if possible, stay at the edges of woodland where there is a degree of cover. Sport hunters typically flush them into the air with beaters or dogs because they consider it unsporting to shoot them while they are not in flight. Since you are hunting for the stew pot, I would advise shooting the animal on the ground. Aim for the centre of the chest for a clean kill. The flavour of a pheasant is not dissimilar to chicken although the meat is drier and tougher.

Deer are mostly active at twilight and they are typically very shy of humans; they have good reason. You are unlikely to be able to get close to deer and so any shots will be at longer range and in poor light. Deer move quickly and prefer being in areas with a fair bit of cover which makes the shot even more difficult. You will need broad headed arrows for this as sporting arrows are unlikely to give you a rapid kill. Even with the right arrow, you are very unlikely to hit the animal's heart and it will run off after being shot. You will probably need to track the injured deer for some distance. Deer stay in family units for the most part and it is not unknown for a buck (male deer) to attack anyone approaching an injured doe. Deer meat is dark red and has a texture like lean beef although the gamey flavour is not as appealing to some.

When hunting, it is important to remember that there may be zombies or hostile survivors in the area.

You may also find cattle that have become feral. Bulls are both dangerous and territorial and they will attack a human that is encroaching on their territory. They are also protective of their harem. Be aware that startled cattle can stampede. Care must be taken even when hunting cows. Being larger animals, they are much more difficult to bring down with a bow. Sheep can be hunted and it is less likely that the ram will be much of a threat. However, their woolly coats can provide a surprising amount of protection against arrows.

Without refrigeration, meat will spoil in a few days. It can be salted to preserve it or made into thin strips and dried. This is a popular option in southern Africa where it is called Biltong. It is something of an acquired taste but will provide protein through the winter.

To make Biltong, soak the meat in vinegar prior to drying. While still wet, roll it in salt and pepper and air dry until it becomes leathery. Only lean meat is suitable for salt drying as the fat will otherwise become rancid. The meat is again cut into thin strips and soaked in water with a 14% salt concentration (5 litres of water will require 810 grams of salt) for 5 minutes. The strips are then hung up to dry. Alternatively, thin strips of meat can be smoked over a fire which will both preserve and flavour them. The wood of fruit trees or oak will produce good results. Pine and any form of treated wood should be avoided.

As soon as possible after death, the animal should be dressed. This is done by opening the abdomen of the animal and removing all internal organs. It is important not to lacerate the gut of the animal while doing this as this contains bacteria that will taint the meat. If your arrow has ruptured the gut of the animal, at least that part of the animal should be discarded. Care should be taken while doing this if the smell of blood is thought likely to attract zombies. It will attract feral dogs.

Before I leave the subject of animals, I would like to mention the roles of cats and dogs. Cats make good pets and can raise morale within your team. They can also be useful in keeping the mouse and rat population of your new home to a reasonable level. They will need feeding if there are not many suitable prey animals for them to hunt and eat. Cats are obligate carnivores; they must eat meat or fish because they are unable to synthesise Taurine, an organic acid not found in vegetable sources. While there is some Taurine in milk, adult cats are generally lactose intolerant and should not be given dairy. Dogs can tolerate a wider range of foods although they do find some compounds such as theobromine (found in tea and chocolate), oxalic acid (found in tomatoes) and grapes or raisins to be highly toxic. They can synthesise Taurine and so can survive on a vegetarian diet although they will not thrive on it. They are less good at hunting mice than cats but typically better at catching and fighting rats, especially smaller breeds such as terriers. They are also good for team morale.

While large dogs could be trained to fight zombies, I do not recommend this for several reasons. The first is that they will not be especially effective although they would be able to do more damage to Sprinters than Shamblers. The second is that they are likely to carry infection back to you and your team after biting a zombie. Even if they are not themselves affected, they could still be a vector for infection. Finally, if they are trained to attack things that look like humans, there is a chance that they will attack humans including you and your team. Dogs have an excellent sense of smell, can be trained to track and have a natural tendency to guard an area being territorial by nature. You may want to keep a few dogs around the compound to provide warning if the lookout does not notice anyone or anything approaching. Given that you do not need the dogs to face zombies in combat, I would suggest that you choose smaller dogs and muzzle them when there is any risk of infection being present. They eat less but are just as territorial, just as good at sounding an alarm and they are better ratters.

You should also give careful consideration to raising a hive of bees. While they require some looking after, can sting and are at risk from diseases peculiar to bees, honey will be a most welcome addition to your diet and is useful if you have to dress wounds.

Power

It will not be practical to run a diesel or petrol generator for long since fuel will spoil and you will need to make multiple foraging trips to bring back additional fuel. However, solar cells will continue to give you limited amounts of power for many years. The main argument against using solar cells (technically, photovoltaic cells) is their cost which ceases to be an issue after Z-day. You will want to fit as many panels of cells as possible to the structure or structures that you live in. The most common type is the amorphous panel – crystalline panels are more efficient but also more expensive and so less common.

Solar panels come in different sizes ranging from 10 watt (very small) to 200 watt (very large) and they are normally chained together to produce a useful level of voltage and current. You can think of the voltage of as the pressure of the electricity and the current as the amount of electricity flowing and resistance as how difficult it is for the electricity to get through something. If there is a lot of pressure, you can push a lot current through a resistance. Solar cells generate DC (direct current) power which can be fed into batteries to charge them. These are similar to car batteries in a lot of ways. The DC power has to be adjusted to the correct voltage (12 V DC) and this is done by a specialised bit of equipment called the controller. The batteries feed into a thing called an inverter that converts the 12 V DC to the 240 V AC (alternating current) that mains powered equipment expects.

The details of how to install these systems vary considerably by model but if, during your foraging, you find a supplier of solar energy systems then you should be able to find installation manuals. You should recover as much equipment of this type as is practical in order to have a sustained and sustainable power supply. Unlike a normal installation, you will not be linking into the national grid to supply power back into the system and you will be limited to the power that you can supply from sunlight falling on the panels. If you cover the entire roof of all buildings, this will be a considerable amount of power – several KW during long summer days. While there is less sunlight and therefore less power available in the winter, it should be possible to keep a refrigerator and a radio running more or less constantly. As with all resources, power should be conserved as much possible to avoid draining the batteries.

Another option for power is a wind turbine with units available that produce 240V AC by means of an embedded inverter. A small turbine can generate 2.4 KW with larger domestic units available in 5 KW or 11 KW versions. Obviously, these only provide power when there is wind above 4 meters per second (about 7 miles per hour). For most of the UK, the average wind speed is 6-7 metres per second and so unless your home is in a very sheltered location, you should get power for much of the time. It is possible to run one of these in parallel with a solar system and this should give enough electrical power for all practical needs. The wind is lowest in the months with the longest days and highest in the months with the shortest days and so a combined approach is likely to offer a reasonably reliable supply. A larger turbine will cost around £30,000 but there will be a very significant discount after Z-day. They are not especially difficult to fit but you will need to study the installation manual for that model and the turbines do require solid foundations. There are relatively few companies that import or make these and you will certainly need a foraging trip with a large vehicle to recover them. Fortunately, the companies that produce these are not in city centres.

Work

There will be two types of work. The work on improving the settlement that you have created is going to be constant but dull and comfortable enough in a hard way. Everyone will have to do what they can. There will also be foraging trips to get what you need. These will be dangerous but vital.

In order to keep your team as happy as possible, jobs should be allocated as fairly as possible. Everyone can cook or learn to cook and everyone should take a turn. Anyone can clean and everyone should. Everyone can plant and weed and everyone should. There will be specialist jobs that only a few of the team will have the skills or the physical attributes to do but those team members should do at least some of the other jobs so that they are not exceptions and so they know how hard the work is for the others. The task rota should be kept somewhere visible and everyone should know what duties others have done. The leader should make a point of doing these tasks willingly, even if it is cleaning the latrine. It is the way to make a team into a family, if not of blood then of shared experience. The work will be hard but it will be necessary and it will certainly be better than starving or freezing outside of the safety of the compound.

Governance

There are many things that we will need to learn to live without in the days following the zombie apocalypse. For most people, their actions will have been constrained by society and their own sense of morality. People have varying degrees of morality and, when society is largely gone, a degree of control on people will have been lost. It is very likely that your survivors will contain a high proportion of strong willed individuals as the will to survive is an asset that will have made them survivors. For the good of the group, there need to be restrictions placed on individuals and, in a world with no police and no organised religion, this is a burden that falls on your community. This will not be easy.

It is useful to have a set of basic rules that are explicitly stated and understood by everyone in the group. While the details may vary, this is a widely applicable set that should suit every community:

1. Acts of violence against other members are prohibited. Obviously, this covers all forms of attack including rape.
2. Acts that needlessly endanger other members are prohibited. When on foraging trips, it will be necessary for members of your team to be put in positions where they are at risk; for example, a lookout covering the team while they investigate a building is clearly in danger of attack. However,

this rule covers offences such as breaking quarantine, leaving a gate unsecured or moving out of position to forage when the team member is guarding the rest of the group. If the offender simply ran away because they were scared, that should be a mitigating factor. However, it should also be a factor considered when assigning roles to them in the future.

3. Wasting resources through negligence. An example of this might be killing a food crop by failing to water them or causing a fire within the compound.

4. Refusing to work. Your community cannot tolerate anyone who is trying to get a free ride. Everyone must do what they can.

5. Theft. There is likely to be little personal property. Most possessions will be held in common; vehicles, weapons and pots and pans belong to everyone. However, what few personal possessions people have will certainly be more precious because of this.

Penalties will depend on the offence. The ultimate penalty is expulsion from the group. Lesser penalties will include shunning, extra work duties, shaming and removal of privileges. The death penalty is probably not one that you want to adopt for several reasons. In a world where humans are endangered, killing anyone works against the species. It is also likely to be unpopular with the group. While all members of the team will be hardened to death by this time, it is an unreasonable emotional burden to place on the executioner. In practice, expulsion is likely to result in the death of the offender, especially if they are not provided with any equipment but there are important differences in terms of the impact on the emotional wellbeing of the group. Failure to accept a penalty is very dangerous to the running of the community. In medieval times, one who rejected the rule of law was considered to be without the protection of the law; they were considered outlaws. Expulsion from the group is going to be the only reasonable penalty for anyone who refuses the rules of the group. Any who are excluded and who survive are very likely to hold a grudge against the group. A wise leader will want to avoid this. This will influence the equipment that you allow the outcast

One important decision that must be made is that of who will judge if an offence has been committed and what penalty should be imposed. There are only really two approaches here. The leader can set themselves up as judge and jury or a group can be formed from within the community to discuss and decide on a course of action. If the leader decides, he or she will make enemies and must take every opportunity to demonstrate fairness. If the community decides then the group should be as large as reasonable and should exclude those who would obviously be biased – if Bob has a broken nose after a fight with Tom then neither Bob nor Tom should decide on who is at fault.

One point that must not be forgotten is that the leader is not only bound by the rules, he or she must be the definition of obedience to the rules. A leader who does not have the respect of the community cannot be an effective leader.

For matters other than disciple, as discussed in chapter 7, a leader should always be willing to listen but ultimately must be responsible for any decisions made that affect the safety and wellbeing of the community. However, routine tasks such as deciding work rotas probably should be decided by a second in command and be subject to leeway so that people will feel that they have at least a degree of control over their lives.

Workshops

In addition to residential space and a quarantine room or two, you will want to have at least a couple of workshops. Since equipment will be difficult to replace, it will be necessary to repair things when possible and create some items within your compound.

Forge/repair shop: Electrical items tend to fail over time, especially when treated roughly. There will certainly be times when moving quickly is going to be higher on your priority list than making sure that a walkie-talkie doesn't get bashed on a door frame. Over time, all manner of things will need to be fixed. It is helpful to have an area for this as small components get lost and some of the equipment is specialised and not useful in other parts of the compound. New items will also need to be made if they cannot be found or if searching for them is dangerous. Ideally, this workshop should have a forge capable of casting and working metal.

While many of the skills of a smith are difficult to master, some are quite simple. Casting metals using the lost wax method is one of these. A replica of the object to be made is created using wax (either bees-wax or paraffin wax) or, if not available, expanded polystyrene of the sort used in packing materials. Because wax is much easier to work than metal or wood, reasonably complex models can be made in this way. The wax (or polystyrene) model will be vaporised when it comes into contact with the molten metal. If the model (called a former) is in the centre of a well dried clay or compressed sand mould, the metal will effectively be encountering a void in the shape of the original model. This allows reasonably detailed castings to be made. If you need multiple copies of an object, you can create a mould to shape the wax former. If the material available to make the mould is not flexible then it will be necessary to warm it to release the wax form. This will result in a little loss of detail and precision. If sand is used as a casting medium then it needs to be both fine and well packed around the former.

There will need to be a hole in the mould to let the liquid metal in, of course. This will fill (at least partially) with metal and this will need to be trimmed off later; the waste metal should be kept since it can be melted down and reused. When the metal and the mould have cooled down, the clay or sand can be broken away from the casting. If there are air bubbles or the metal has not flowed into all of the shape then the metal was probably too cool. If a clay mould shatters, it should have been drier; it takes days to dry. The clay mould can also be gently heated, removing the wax and any moisture prior to use.

The essence of a forge is that it is a hot fire with forced ventilation. Wood will not generally get hot enough but coal, coke or charcoal will do nicely. Petrol stations in rural areas have a small supply of these and charcoal can be made from wood by heating it in a fire that has very little oxygen.

The essential elements are a bellows and an area for the fire. To contain these, you will need fire bricks. Metal will not work for the temperatures that you will be working with and would conduct the heat away too rapidly. Normal bricks will not work well because they will tend to spall (flake) when exposed to that level of heat. Firebricks are something of a specialist item found in places that build and sell fireplaces but they can be salvaged from an old fireplace if that is all that is available. They will not be as tough as the bricks used in kilns and forges normally are but they will survive much better than normal brick.

To build your forge:

1. Create a bed of firebricks. Use a cement with a high level of sand as this will be more resistant to the heat. The bricks should be as close together as possible.
2. Build the walls at the sides to a height of about 18 inches.
3. Fit bricks to the back of the forge, forming a 3 sided box. You will probably need to cut several bricks to make a good fit. You will need to leave or drill a gap to allow the bellows to blow into the fire box that you have created.
4. Lay bricks across the top giving you a low box with one side open. Leave or cut a gap to form a vent in the top to allow smoke to escape without going through the front of the forge.
5. Add a single brick at the bottom front of the forge making the box more enclosed.
6. If you have a suitable steel tray, you can insert it into the forge bed to collect ash. It will be easier than raking it out by hand.

The simplest form of bellows is a tube of leather that feeds into a metal pipe at one end and is open at the other. You will need to install two 1 foot long wooden handles so that they will be vertical when the bellows are in place and attach the leather to the handles on both sides. The effectively gives you a leather bag that you can open and close by pushing the handles together or pulling them apart. By opening the bag to let air in, closing it and pushing the air out of the bag (thrusting forwards), you force air into the forge.

The forge fire will need kindling (small bits of wood, paper etc.) on the bottom and charcoal, coke or coal as available. Metal that you will be hammering can sit directly on the coals while metal that you are casting will need to go in a ceramic dish capable of withstanding the high temperatures. It will need a good deal of practice to know the heat of the metal by the colour that it glows but it is possible to tell after a while.

The following metals are listed in order of melting point:

Tin	214 C
Lead	327 C
Aluminium	660 C
Brass	920 C
Bronze	950 C
Silver	961 C
Gold	1063 C
Copper	1085 C
Iron	1538 C
Tungsten	3400 C

Steel will melt at different temperatures depending on what it is alloyed with. A forge of the type above will be able to soften iron and possibly melt it. Tungsten will not be workable since the highest attainable temperature will be in the order of 1900 C.

Shaping metal with a hammer is a skill that can only be learned with practice. When cooling metals, the speed of cooling makes a significant difference to the properties of the metal because it alters the crystal size. Water will quickly cool the piece and it will harden it but there is a risk of the worked metal cracking. Oil will cool the metal more slowly making it less hard but also less brittle. Allowing the metal to cool slowly in air gives a softer metal that will tend to bend rather than break.

Brewery: Monks brewed beer to make water safe to drink and we can follow their example as long as we don't overdo it. To make an alcoholic beverage, you need water, yeast and some form of sugar. There are literally thousands of recipes and what you brew will largely depend on what you have available. You will need to get all of your equipment as close to sterile as you can make it. If you can boil it, do boil it. If you cannot then wash it will boiling water. You will need a tub or barrel with a close fitting lid that has a hole in the top and a hose that you can connect to the hole.

For cider: Take a quantity of apples (you can use pears but then you will have a perry rather than a cider). Crush them to get as much of the juice out as possible. Sieve the juice through a cloth and then put the pulp in the cloth and get as much of the remaining juice out as possible. The pulp will be edible and sweet so don't waste it. There are natural yeasts on the skins of apples in small quantities. Put the juice in the barrel or bin. Attach the hose and arrange it so that part of it forms a "u" shape. Add some boiled water into that section of hose as this makes a simple airlock; the gases will bubble through the water if the hose is of a reasonable size. Fermentation should start in 1-2 days. You will know when it has because you will hear the bubbles of escaping carbon-dioxide. Additional apple juice can be added later – the sugars in the juice will help to keep fermentation going. The temperature should be kept as constant as possible and around 20 degrees is ideal. When fermentation is complete, replace the hose with a bung to seal it and allow the cider to mature for several months. When it has matured, you can decant it into bottles (sterilised as best possible) or simply drunk.

Beers are more difficult as you will have to make a wort which is a mash of grain and water and typically the grain is toasted to add flavour. However, pretty much anything that contains sugar can be fermented and some experimentation will tell you which were the most enjoyable.

If a batch goes bad then the likely cause is poor sterilisation of the equipment.

Vinegar can be made out of any alcoholic drink by letting it go sour. Alternative, anything containing alcohol can be distilled to create neat alcohol.

Distillery: Sadly, this is not for fine whiskeys but to create alcohol for cleaning wounds and other uses. While this could be used to create drinks, strong spirits are not very compatible with living in a hostile environment. The essence of a still is simple. There is an effectively sealed chamber where the liquid is heated; this is called a cooker and it is normally a metal or glass vessel with a single vent that connects to the worm. The worm is a long pipe where the distillate can condense. Coils of thin copper pipe have traditionally been used for this purpose, sometimes cooled by a flow of water over them. Old refrigerators are a good source for that sort of pipe.

There are some dangers associated with distilling alcohol. The first is that the pressure in the cooker can get sufficiently high that it can explode. The best way to avoid that is to have a bung that can blow out rather than shattering the cooker. The second risk is that the ethanol can be broken into methanol which is even more toxic than ethanol. While this is still perfectly suitable for sterilising things, it will cause harm if drunk. To avoid this, the mixture in the cooker should remain below 78 C. A jam making thermometer is useful for ensuring this.

The still can also be used to create very pure water which is useful for a number of purposes.

The library: Ultimately, this will prove to be the most important room in the house.

While you should certainly keep a record of the founding of this safe place in an unsafe land, the majority of the information that you keep here will have to be foraged for... fortunately, looters will have left libraries alone for the most part and there would have been little there to interest zombies. While it does require a trip into a town (which, as discussed, is dangerous), it is essential that you salvage the knowledge that our culture created over hundreds of generations.

I cannot tell you what to consider as art worth saving; that is something that you will have to decide for yourself. However, there are techniques and skills that may no longer exist anywhere outside of a library. If mankind is to avoid a new dark ages, we must preserve all that we can of what we had. In the end, gold has no real value and rubies are just shiny stones. The truest treasure is knowledge and you must keep it safe for your children and their children after them. You will certainly want the sciences and some works of history but there will be more than you can possibly take in a single trip. For your first visit, I would suggest that you concentrate on the more urgent and practical needs. Since the library will be arranged according to the Dewey Decimal system, I have listed some topics that will probably be of immediate interest:

Medicine	610-618
Blacksmithing	682
Brewing	663
Archery, fletching, bowmaking	799.3
Beekeeping	638.1
Animal husbandry	636
Leatherworking	675
Electronics repair	620
Weapons	623.4
Wildcraft	338.1
Woodworking	684

When you return, you should take a good sampling of the 500s since all of the hard sciences are there. If you crave religion, it is in the 200s. History is to be found at 900. Literature is spread through the low 800s. In the end, you and others like you will decide what knowledge must be saved and what can be lost. You will be looking at a culture that has come and gone and so perhaps your view will be more objective than mine. I hope that you choose well.

I do have a small favour to ask of you. This book is not a great work of literature but I hope that it has helped you to survive the rise of the zombie and the fall of man. If it comes to pass that you are salvaging the collected works of humanity, please make a little room for this book, slight though it is compared to the work of others.

When you have done all that is needed, you will have created a safe and sustainable home for you and those who have worked alongside you. This is not a small task. It is not a task with an end as there will always be more to do.

It is a great and wonderful thing and you did it yourself.

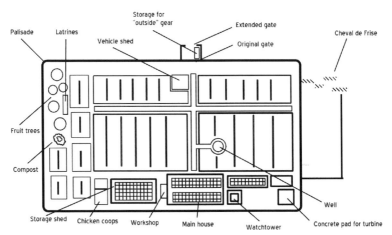

This is a well established compound. The land slopes down towards the gate and the majority of the ground is covered by fields divided into strips. The well has been dug nearer to the house but well outside of the foundations. The smithy is on the side of the house to allow excess heat to escape. The compost heap is near the latrines to allow transfer of solid wastes. The fruit trees planted next to the latrines take advantage of the richer soil. It should be noted that the latrines are downslope from the well. The watch tower is close to the house which has the disadvantage that noise from the house could mask sounds from outside the compound but has the advantage that people in the house could hear an alarm raised in the tower. The house, the storage shed (originally a barn) and a purpose built quarantine block all have solar panels installed. A pad has been installed for a turbine which is currently in the shed waiting for construction. The original gate has been extended to form an area for cleaning the vehicle and team members returning from trips outside. The defences are in the process of being modified to include an area to the right hand side. The palisade has had a gate added and now leads into a new area that will be cultivated. The palisade of the new section is not yet complete and temporary defences have been added to protect the team members working on enclosing the area.

12. What next?

What happens next is life. There will be work and there will be leisure time. Babies will get born and people will need to teach them. You will need to develop a new society, one in which there are fewer people and without many of the things that we had before. In time, villages and towns may be reclaimed although we will not need the cities for many years to come. We will need to master the art of small living.

In a perfect world, none of the things that I described will have come to pass. Unfortunately, we live in an imperfect world. If you are reading this in your compound and you have lived through Z-day and the weeks and years that followed then I salute you. You have an expertise won by hard experience that far exceeds my own conjecture. I hope that these words have helped you along the way and that any mistakes that I have made did not cost you too dearly.

The future will belong to you, the others who have survived and to your children. You will have to bring them up in a very different world.

We can raise them to work hard and take pleasure in a job well done. The best way that we can teach this is by having them join us in those tasks. They will learn by doing and they will learn the value of working together. They will need to learn a great deal more and the books that you have preserved will be their teachers if we can help them to have enquiring minds.

Humanity is starting over and we will be the same naked apes that we always were but perhaps we can learn to live better with each other and with nature.

Some things will have to be very different about the new world that you create. The world is not the place of our ancestors. Most of the oil is gone. The remaining coal is far underground and the mines will have deteriorated. The ores are mostly worked out. Our children will have to learn to want only what is truly needful.

There may be even more profound changes needed. A small community does not offer the genetic diversity that a race needs to be healthy. We will need to mix with other survivors and see a stranger not as another face to be ignored but as someone that we must welcome. In this new world, we must learn to share what resources there are and give what we are able.

What happens next is life.

About the author, thanks and acknowledgements

I rather feel that I cheated while writing this book. Rather than doing a great deal of research, I wrote down the things that I have learned by thinking and reading about these problems for a number of years. In a sense, all of my adult life has been research.

I was also fortunate in my background. Without going into detail, I have a background in crisis management. I have had training in risk assessment, risk reduction and disaster recovery, all of which helped. I come from a military family and much of what I learned from my father was useful here. My current job involves asking the question "What is the worst possible case?" over and over and again.

I have also played and written roleplaying scenarios for more than 30 years. If you are familiar with them, I need not explain but in case you are not, they involve getting together with friends to problem solve your way through hundreds of different scenarios. Serious men who work for serious governments do this for money but we did it for fun. It is, I have to say, splendid training for handling the unexpected.

Much of my knowledge of how to treat wounds and infection prevention is due to training that I received from St John Ambulance. I do not speak for the organisation.

You may wonder why I wrote this book. Is it because I really expect a zombie apocalypse? Well, it is not impossible as I said in the book. Is it likely? Perhaps not. However, knowing what you would do and what resources you have within you is of value in its own right. Z-day is the worst case emergency but there are many other things that could happen. If you are prepared for the worst, you can handle anything else with comparative ease. One critical thing that I hope that you will have discovered is that there are always things that you can do to help yourself survive no matter how bad the crisis.

Thank you for reading this. I would also like to extend my thanks to others who have helped me to write this book:

Southern Water for their advice.

My test readers.

Emma Crowe for asking all the difficult questions.

Kymberlee Price for encouragement and introducing me to Shane.

Talis Kimberley for corrections and advice on sustainable communities.

The Centre for Disease Control.

My editor, Professor Roxanne Brennan.

My illustrator, Shane Feazell.

Ian Peters for odds and ends.

All mistakes in this book belong to me. Much that is correct, I owe to the people above.

Printed in Great Britain
by Amazon